A
SET
OF
LINES

A SET OF LINES

S. D. Stewart

Illustrations by Nate Dorr

Cover and Illustrations © 2020 by Nate Dorr
natedorr.com

Layout by Nathan Grover
nathangrover.com

Published by Ghost Paper Archives
ghostpaperarchives.com

ISBN: 978-1-7349390-0-2 (pbk.)

For Chris R.

VOLUME I

PROLOGUE

I left the house that day in a daze. The air was hot and close. I remember I was wearing jean shorts and a gingham shirt I had knotted above my waist. I see myself leave the house, the screen door slamming behind me, my mother screaming again. Now I'm in the strip of woods behind the block, walking toward your house, the crunch of last year's leaves filling my ears.

Breathing in the resinous scent around me, I walk slower, my limbs leaden, moving with jerky automaton motion. I hold the paper in my hand. No, I had jammed it in the pocket of my shorts before leaving the house. Don't slam that door! Mama had shouted. Last night I drew all night. I copied the images from the textbook and then I drew them again freehand—I made them move on the page, lengthened the lines and darkened the centers. I'm excited to show you.

It feels cooler in the woods, out of the sun. I see the tree ahead. I long to run my hands along its smooth bark, to find its mossy center with my fingers and claim it for my own, thirsting for the roots deep in the black earth.

I am near your yard now. I can see you through the trees. I slide my hand into my pocket, push at the fabric and the paper crinkles, the pressure of my fingers urgent on my thigh.

The clouds are moving in but the fading sun still falls down through the trees, falls on you standing there in the center of the bowl-shaped yard. I step out of the woods. You turn your head toward me then quickly back to the house. I feel light, floating—my head gauzy with mist. I see my feet below me in tennis shoes, no socks, moving like pale slugs across the grass.

The grass is electric green and I see the blades, each one swaying erect in the breeze. There is a rhythm to their movement and I feel the rhythm slither forward and up my legs, shifting my hips as I walk toward you. You turn back to me again and I smile, reaching for my pocket...

1.

Imperfection loves a perfect set of lines, smooth and angled yet broken down the middle, dark and center-tangled. Look at this, she had said. But he didn't know what it meant. Uncertain heat felt on the rim of this disused quarry, excavated with care then abandoned before mining began. The differing needs, down there for one, up here for another. And now there is this in between, only finding the desperation of a day's end.

When she showed it to him his thoughts were redacted. So much of that time masked off in his mind. But perhaps if he resolved this end-of-day situation there might be hope. There were distractions, of course, but they were of minor consequence.

Before the end-of-day dread there was only what she'd shown him in the fading light. Look at this, she had said. The tree with the orange bark floated in the mist filling his head. There was no end to this mist.

At work so much of what was coming in these days was garbled. The hers and the hims. Hes and shes. Squares of people filling a screen sitting atop artificial wood grain. Madness! (He took her by the hand, led her to the tree with orange bark...no, no, that's not what happened.) Connection drops: another thing on his mind. No one seemed capable of preventing them. It could be related to the end-of-day dread, a predictor of the switch flipping off in his head.

Down there, down there, she urged.

Floating, floating, he was floating. He saw his hands doing things, furtive things, but felt nothing. He was standing motionless on the grass. He was standing next to the tree. There was no motion. The air was still. *It's just a picture, a mental image.*

During a lull in processing he went to the coffeehouse, where he found E smoking an electronic cigarette, the unscented vapor escaping from her lips and obscuring her features. She could be anyone. But there was the blue hair. That did set her apart.

Back at the office dozens of messages were coming in now. He had to concentrate. *Delete, delete, forward, reply, reply all, delete.* Mostly deletions today. *I am like the Censor now.* He deleted for the rest of the day, until the dread rose up, a funnel cloud of a thousand demon faces. *Hello demons, how nice to see you again. It's time to leave this place.*

Screen blackout mode at his quarters—just as well. In rapid succession he read 10 pages in each of the six books he was currently reading. He did not think about what she had shown him. Despite what he had felt, was it shock, confusion, heat...what was it. After a good night of sleep he recorded his dreams in the book. *New day, new day.*

2.

Shorter days made the endings come sooner, bleaker. He met E again for coffee. She was not smoking. He wanted to tell her about what had been shown to him so long ago, and what it had done, but even he was not sure if that had been the cause. It was a vignette in his head, a fixed image sometimes moving. Besides, today she did not seem amenable to anecdotes from him. Now she was smoking while scraping at her chipped nail polish. His eyes moved vaguely across her face. *Down there, down there.*

I must get back to work, he announced.

He stood and waved his arm toward the door, the one no one used anymore.

Her eyes followed and she laughed. You work out there?

He gazed out the window to his right. High winds blasted grit against the thick glass. A weak grey light of no visible source illuminated nothing but vague shapes glimpsed during pauses in the storm.

Of course not, he muttered.

She rose and they walked together into the tunnel. At the Y he paused at the right tube as she strode into the left one.

Goodbye, her voice floated back to him.

For the next several weeks he left work earlier by a series of tiny, increasing increments each day. This didn't solve the problem, as his mind noted the difference, recalculated, and sent the updated information to his body, which tensed up according to the new time...*the smoke, the demons.* Everything adjusted, so he returned to normal routine. *Normal.*

The scene always arrived with no warning. The urgency in her voice as she pressed the paper into his hand. No, wait, he remembered now she hadn't spoken. He was putting words in her mouth. *Down there, down there.* Had she written it on the paper? The paper was damp. Clutched in her hand. He could no longer picture her face. He looked down at her, then away. She was standing to his left. Maybe she had pointed. Yes, maybe that was it. She hadn't said anything, but had pointed. Nothing was written on the paper. Just her "artwork." He laughed. It sounds so ridiculous now.

At work the money was coming in fast. Bundles of it, millions of credits. None of it funneled down, of course. He stared at the screen. Faces inside squares— were they real people? Most days he didn't think about it. Just *reply, delete, reply all, forward, wait for response, click check-boxes, click submit, arrows, buttons, approve this, decline that, connection drop.* Go see E at the coffeehouse. That's where he was now. She was trying to quit e-cigarettes. It wasn't pretty.

Have you gone to that new club? she snapped.

He stared at her over the rim of his coffee cup. She had her hair pulled back—the blue ran straight down the middle, like a skunk's stripe. Imperfection loves a perfect set of lines. He glanced down, an imperceptible glance, or so he thought.

No, I haven't gone to the club. I no longer go in the tunnels at night.

But she had seen his glance. Well, well.

He returned to his quarters that night and put something ambient on the turntable. Drank a glass of scotch. He had to be more careful. The Censor was around. Or was it. Years ago he was supposedly freed from its control, but the paranoia remained. He tried to recall the image of a body of water. The shimmering light as the water moved. The tree with the orange bark. Was it on the shore...no, it was in the woods behind the house. He had led her there to show it to her. No, that's not right. He'd gone alone, after she left. Mood affects memory. These meetings with E made him manic. What if he placed her in front of the cloud...*the smoke, the demons.*

He woke up still sitting in front of the sun lamp. Checked his vitamin D level with the meter. It was high, very high. He felt good. *Maybe I should sleep in front of it every night.*

3.

The concept of "daytime" was no longer relevant. Of course the yard that day had been lush with greenery. So long ago and yet still feels like present in his mind. A moving portrait. The beginnings of a lifelong struggle, trudging that perpetual circuit around the quarry's rim. She showed it to him and left the yard, walking down the narrow path next to the house. Or did she cut through the neighbor's yard. Had anyone seen her? He wondered. Not that anything had happened. She merely showed him the paper and he looked away. Confused heat in his head—a new feeling. Wait, had he kept it. No, no, he gave it back to her. Or maybe he hadn't even held it, just glanced at it and turned away. The Censor had been watching from the window. Redacted. So much redaction.

E was staring at him.

What's wrong with you today?

He looked around, his eyes passing across her face. Imperfection loves a perfect set of lines, center-tangled.

Sorry, I'm just distracted.

She chewed her nicotine gum with gusto. It's more than that today, I'm afraid. I suspect you've been spending too much time alone again.

He sipped his coffee. Well, work is...you know, the messages, processing credits.

She stood up. I don't care about your work. Why can't you ever just talk to me, you know, about *yourself.*

He thought she was going to leave but in fact only went to refill her cup. His mind had already adjusted to the actuality of her departure, made the necessary shifts in thinking, calculating, recalculating. He watched her walk back to the table, as the heads of everyone else in the shop turned toward her.

He returned to the office for the meta-meeting, the one where they discussed all the other meetings. It was the one he hated most of all. He kept his wireless earphones in and listened to electronica while trying to sync the beats with the moving lips around him. His pen tapped his notebook in time. No one addressed him, nor did he speak. He simply lost an hour of processing.

The clients on the other side of the globe whose day ended during the meeting would have to wait until their tomorrow, which would dawn while he was living in his dreams.

Walking in the tunnels after work he recalled the paper had been damp. So he had touched it after all. Perhaps it was damp from her sweaty hand. He thought she'd been holding it as she walked from her house down the street. That would make sense. Today he'd tried to type her name into the machine at work, but realized he only knew her nickname. He'd grown used to typing names in, seeing the rows of faces inside boxes appear, reading the information below the faces and trying to imagine them as three-dimensional real people. It couldn't work with her, even if he knew her true name. She would not look anything like she did on that day. Standing on the green grass, her hand extended, looking up at him. He tried to place the expression on her face, still blurred in his mind. Expectant, perhaps. She was probably a couple of years younger than him. He should have been the one who knew better. But there had been the Censor, the incessant redactions, so much time alone, and now... *the smoke, the demons.*

He reached the ladder, eased open the hatch, climbed out into the lobby of his building. There was no mail worth more than a glance. He threw the circulars in the green bin. The elevator was silent. The entire building was silent. *Does anyone even live here?* How could everyone else be on a completely different schedule. It didn't make sense. He looked around. There were numbers on all the doors, so there should be people behind them. He placed his palm against the door across the hall, palpating for vibrations. He felt nothing. He thought about afternoons by the river. It seemed like a different life. *What we have now feels arbitrary.*

It was a simple transaction. She handed him something, showed it to him. Maybe she didn't intend for him to keep it or to even hold it. Maybe it was a suggestion, an invitation. Yes, it had felt that way...a source of his confusion. A confusion still present after all these years. He pushed open the door to his quarters and left it to close behind him.

4.

If he tried thinking about how long he had known E his head began to ache. Everything bled out into the sensorium. A decade sounded like a certain album. One year smelled like patchouli, another like tamari and rice vinegar, yet another like cotton candy, it went on and on. A length of time felt like a river, snaking serpentine, always moving, but not always looking or feeling like motion. A series of curving lines, center-tangled. An empty bird's nest resting in the crook of two erect reeds, swaying in salty mesmeric breezes. Of course it was possible he was mad. But he rarely considered it. At this time in history the question seemed irrelevant.

He did wonder why E still insisted on meeting him. For clearly she did suspect him to be mad, and he doubted that held appeal for her. He may have been a conduit to her past, perhaps the only one left. Not that she was one for nostalgia, but rather if she kept him close there was less chance he would use his knowledge to harm her. What she probably didn't know was how useless his memory had become, how vague and unreliable his handle was on the past.

Do you want to walk down to the river? he had asked. No, that's not true. There was no river, not then, not there, not with her. Only the strip of woods behind the houses, where the tree with the orange bark stood, a gaping hole in its middle. He had been there, knew every square inch of that strip of woods: the rotting logs, the rusting junk, the failed treehouse. If it wasn't important, why was it still there so clear, humming with urgency in his mind.

At work he was now processing up to 500 requests each day. During idle moments he forced himself to think about E and when he had first met her. It must have been around the time he was released from the "care" of the Censor, a blurry period in his head, for even though the redactions had ceased, there were residual effects. A caul covered his mind for several years and recall was spotty. Around the time he entered university, perhaps. And during this time he must have met E, whose hair was not yet blue. Imperfection loves a pair of swaying reeds, center-tangled. He had to stop traveling back before a migraine seized him.

In the tunnels featureless blobs moved past him, all of them in a hurry. He wondered if any of them lived in his building. Not once had he encountered anyone else in the lobby. Yet the building felt alive to him. *I do not feel lonely. And yet I am alone.* The green grass, the sun streaming through the oak leaves, her hand extended, her small delicate hand. He felt an ache. *Down there, down there.* Pushing him to the quarry's edge with her voice—the sound of an urgency to share.

For years he'd searched covertly for the Censor, in between processing, poring over pirated government documents scraped from the dark web, but to no avail. Not surprising considering their status as revered stewards of society. *We will honor our Censors to the death, protect them from harm.* He wondered how many others were like him: impaired, limping through life, tormented by what little had not been redacted. Had it been an error to leave those scraps behind? Is that how the others managed to live the way they did, free of his kind of burden. Had the Censor wronged him more than was intended? This tiny cracked window he was forced to squint through, maybe it was all a simple administrative error, like when he missed a check-box while processing. He couldn't bear to think about it, and yet he wanted to ask E what she knew.

5.

Some nights he slept and other nights he did not. He knew it was morning only by the chirping of the artificial birds. The light outside his opaque windows never changed. It was a constant dull grey, useful for nothing. He checked his vitamin D. Normal. There was none of the euphoria from the other day, the other week, the other month, whenever he had last felt "good." Overnight he had dreamed about the paper, what was on it, hieroglyphics he could not decipher. But he had felt the same heat in his face that he recalled in waking life. A dream world without Censors.

An image of E arose in his head, from that blurry time, must have been at university. There was something in her gaze, not of this world, and not even a visible flicker of interest in him. If he still had the paper he could show it to her and ask her opinion. He felt sure there was a connection to be made there. He felt it, this barest sensation, from years of probing at the jagged edges of the redactions in his mind. Lifting the corners to feel what breathed out. His Censor in certain ways had been sloppy. Weak seals riddled its work. There was this memory and whether it should exist in his mind, if it even belonged to him, or whether it was even a memory at all.

Work was tapering off now. His division was entering the slow time. The managers were busy distributing the recent inflow of credits, giving themselves promotions, hiring new personal assistants, ordering new hardware. Meanwhile, his machine trembled on the artificial wood grain, plagued by connection drops. He doubted a flaw in the machine, a recent model. But the entire building had been rewired by the lowest bidder on a sub-contract. When he looked up the contractor online there was no evidence of the company ever existing. Just another credit vulture the managers hadn't bothered vetting. What did he care. So long as the credits kept appearing in his account twice per month, he would never object. *Delete, delete, reply, forward, scan, scroll down, click submit...*the smoke, the demons.

Now in the coffeehouse he sat across from E meditating on her facial structure, the lines, the angles.

I see what you're doing.

What am I doing?

She smiled. You're deconstructing my face into a set of lines, reducing me to a mathematical equation that will make sense to you.

He shifted his gaze to the gaudy holiday decorations encroaching on their table from every possible direction.

Well, am I right?

He shifted in his seat. You have good bone structure.

What does that mean?

Well, you know how there are these studies where subjects are shown human faces and their physical responses are recorded.

She frowned. No, I don't know.

So, the conclusions point to a biological reason for beautiful people receiving preferential treatment in life.

Why is that?

I'm not sure exactly. Something in the brain causes us to be more likely to react in a positive way to a "beautiful" person than to a less attractive one. As humans we have an unconscious desire to appease beauty. It has to do with symmetry, I think. Anyway, I believe your face fits the profile.

She stared at him.

Mine does not, he added.

She stood up and again he thought she was going to leave. [Readjust, shrink inward, create distance around himself.] But, no, she was refilling her cup. He averted his eyes from her return trip.

The smoke and demons followed him into the tunnels. He felt them wrapping wraith-like around him, enveloping him in a damp unease. Hurrying into the lobby of his building, he forgot to check the mail and rushed into the elevator with relief. Entering his hallway, he thought he saw furtive movement at the very end and then nothing. The doors made no noise when closing so he couldn't say if it was another tenant returning, or if he had imagined it. He felt oppressed but he couldn't say why. Peering into the quarry from its narrow rim, at the machinery now rusting in that abandoned pit. Emptiness began to spread across his chest. He heard the urgency of her voice clanging in his head. *Down there, down there.*

6.

Some days he pushed at the ache inside while other days he ignored it. He thought of the river, of a cloud-stippled sky, of the psithurism that formerly ushered in the autumnal approach. He recalled how the loss of leaves revealed empty nests from the season before. In the first years after the so-called Change he struggled with the absence of seasonal cycles. He resisted the artificial maintenance of his circadian rhythms. But his life soon devolved into haunted havoc. His work suffered and he was almost released due to poor performance. He remembered now how one day E had come to his quarters after he had not been to the coffeehouse for days. She found him near-catatonic from lack of sleep. After administering melatonin she stayed with him while he slept. When he woke she turned on the sun lamp she had brought and made him breakfast. This is how it is now, she had told him before leaving.

So he made himself adapt. But it was never enough—he always felt like an alien, aloof and alone. The generation after his grew up without a need to adjust. This was all they knew.

Toward the end, before the cities were enclosed, there had been so many Code Red days he had stopped ever leaving the house without his mask on. Maybe this had kept his lungs from the more severe scarring now plaguing much of the older populace. It was difficult to pin survival on any single practice one had chosen to adopt, no matter how calculated it may have seemed at the time. In all likelihood survival had instead been random. This made it even harder to comprehend.

In the morning the tunnels were no less turgid with columns of human flesh. The faceless figures hunched and undulated forward as one being—a many-headed snake, for legs and feet were cloaked in shadow. He shrank from the clammy walls, dripping with dirty grey condensation glinting in the orange glow of the sodium lamps overhead. The only sound was the drops hitting unseen puddles. *Down there, down there.* Sometimes it was a shrieking in his head. Had she grabbed his wrist? But no, he thought there had been no contact. That had always been his position. His position? As if there had been an investigation. But he remembered her as walking away, not running in panic. His face had been hot. And in her eyes, what was in her eyes. He thought she was small for her age, an age close to his but younger, a delicate figure but kind of a tomboy. He had not paid her much mind before that day, the green grass, the clouds stippled overhead. His concerns had lain *in another realm*, or rather they had been *redacted*.

The muddle inside his brain only settled during work hours. When the muddle roiled up again after a day of processing, the end-of-day dread rose with it—effluvium of the past seeping back into his consciousness. Bitter revulsion at this nostalgia melted in the back of his throat as he watched the next day's inevitable sameness projected against the dull backdrop of each late afternoon. Mindless though they were, however, his duties did keep him occupied. And there were the distractions, the faces in the halls much like those in the tunnels, only more familiar. Years of smiling and nodding, yet no wrinkles ever formed. As we forever see ourselves as adolescents in the mirror, the same seemed to be true of these colleagues whose faces he had been staring into for a decade, mechanical in their ageless dispassion.

Today he lingered in the tunnel outside the coffee-house. E sat erect, a reed refusing to sway. Others moved around her yet she took no notice of them. She sipped from her cup, waiting for him. He entered the shop and walked toward her. Her head swiveled toward him. He opened the door of the classroom and her head turned. He was seeing her for the first time and yet she looked familiar to him. She showed no sign of recognition, her eyes grey and inscrutable.

You're late.

He sat down with his coffee. I was tending to last minute requests.

She rolled her eyes. When are you going to leave that awful job?

He shrugged. You know I can't. There is no other work.

She uncrossed and re-crossed her legs, agitated. There is always other work. Your problem is you've become too comfortable.

He remembered he hadn't recorded his dreams that morning. A sudden agitation sprouted from this seed.

I'm never too comfortable.

You know what I mean.

He did not know what she meant, but chose not to press the point. She felt prickly today and he did not want the tips of her thorns broken off beneath his skin. Imperfection loves a perfect set of lines, angled yet broken down the middle, dark and center-tangled. She handed it to him and she walked away. No, she handed it to him and he pushed it away. No, he tore it from her hands, ripped it to shreds. No, he led her to the tree with orange bark. No, he shook his head and ran inside, *ran inside, ran inside.* Yes, to the Censor, always watching, always waiting to administer the strangled comfort of redaction.

He said goodbye to E and they parted ways at the tunnel Y.

7.

He was standing at the tree with orange bark. He reached out with shaking hands to touch the smoothness. The trunk forked near its base and at the fork was a hollow, overgrown with moss. Dark and center-tangled. His hand glided along the smooth curves of the fork, his fingers moving through the soft moss to enter the hollow.

He woke and recorded his dreams in the book. He stared out the opaque window at the never-fading light. He thought about the river, puzzled over the fragments of his life he could recall from before the Change. *Does anyone else think like this or had their Censors completed the job.* He built many lives in his head and destroyed them all before each day was out. But she alone remained, a small hand extended, holding the paper out to him, her eyes imploring him, and the way he turned away, his face hot from the blood surging beneath his skin.

He met E at the coffeehouse. Today she spoke in soothing tones, her abrasion left behind for reasons unknown to him. He took her words inside him and spread them like a salve over all his hidden sores.

Why do you do this to yourself?

I don't have any control over it.

She stared at him with unblinking eyes. Her eyes of a grey unplumbed depth.

Do you remember the river?

He felt himself untethering and reached for the table. His coffee cup rattled in its saucer.

No, I don't. I don't remember the river.

At the office his machine shook violently on the artificial wood grain. The connection drops were getting worse. His fingers clattered across the keyboard, *alt-tab, enter, ctrl-t, ctrl-c, ctrl-v, click check-box, submit, confirm.* Cold-wave pulsed through his headphones as he processed. His supervisor stopped by and he read the man's lips for long enough to determine the need to remove an earphone. He found it difficult to concentrate on this intrusive voice. Something about the new credits, management waste: a familiar whining drone recycled across many project iterations. He smiled and nodded until the man left. Insert earphone, adjust volume, *reply, attach file, reply all, annotate and forward, delete, delete, block sender.*

He genuflected to the twin screens before descending to the tunnels.

It was an old tree. The tree often entered his dreams, not always in the same form but he always knew it. Recognition in dreams was a curious thing. The familiar often took on new and strange forms yet still retained its essence. The ambiguity of waking life dissolved in the dream world. Nothing confused him there. He welcomed the fantastic, the incongruous. It all made sense there, whereas this "existence" he occupied in waking life destroyed him every day. For example, there was no one in the elevator of his building, ever. Perhaps there was a hidden staircase he did not know about. Perhaps no one left the building. Telecommuters. It was not unusual. He was not the only one to detest traveling in the tunnels. Still, to remain in his quarters around the clock would only drive him further into madness. It would be a different kind of stifling.

8.

Nothing should be considered as chance. His reconnection with E. The empty corridors of his building. His machine quaking on the artificial wood grain. The connection drops. The never-changing light, not dim but not bright. The tree with the orange bark with its mossy crevice. Walking to the river. A hand extended. Her hand extended. An imploring look. Her "artwork." The Censor looming over him, its mouth sutured shut and its eyes demon red. Staring him down as he stood at the rim of the quarry, abandoned before mining even began.

He was staring at the muddy brown river. His fingers clattered across the keyboard. *Delete, reply, insert, submit, submit, submit, approve, approve, ctrl-x, ctrl-v.* The river was roiling after a storm. Debris clogged the shoreline. The green grass stained watery brown. He stood on the bank. There was no one around. The sun reflected off the water onto the underside of the bridge above, projecting silvery waves of abstract shimmering motion. He wanted it to mean something. He wanted to dissolve into that light.

In the coffeehouse E stirred her coffee with languor. It mesmerized him.

I remember...things, he began.

She looked up at him with her grey eyes. He felt the heat rise in his face.

What things?

I can't really say.

She stopped stirring. Do you remember it...the river?

He saw the shadows race across the underside of the bridge.

No...no, I don't remember the river.

They finished drinking their coffee in silence.

When they separated at the Y, she touched his arm.

It's hard not to feel this far away, she said. Please keep trying.

He watched her walk away, a reed refusing to sway.

At his quarters that night he opened the dream book. He wondered if it were wise to look for patterns. *Nothing should be considered as chance.* Yes, but who was saying that. He closed the book without reading any of it. He felt his body root down through the green grass beneath his feet. He felt her presence next to him. A small warm being holding something in her extended hand. Her wrist so thin, browned by the summer sun. He remembered the way the yard sloped down to the next yard, a series of ill-conceived terraces separated by a strip of woods. To his right was the back of the house. Was the Censor at the window, he couldn't say for sure. At that age he was less aware of its constant vigilance, though no less a victim of it than he would soon become. The blackness crept in. Redaction.

He crossed the marble floor and descended into the tunnels. Condensation dripping. Murky orange light. Heels striking concrete. The rustle of overcoats. Face-lessness. At his desk drone doom filled his ears. *Reboot, reply, attach file, forward, submit, approve, approve, confirm, click check-boxes.* He didn't hear from E so he went to the coffeehouse and sat alone, next to the window, watching the customers shuffle through the queue. He sipped his coffee while making the necessary calculations in his head. One cup of coffee equaled two credits, 12 people currently in the queue, 24 credits total. He scanned his card on the reader mounted to the wall: he had more than enough credits to purchase one cup of coffee for each customer, if he were to choose to do so. He imagined the reaction were he to approach the queue and announce he was buying everyone coffee. Disbelief, distrust...the nagging sense of a hidden catch. *The idea that nothing worthwhile comes free of charge has been forever burned into us.*

9.

Where was E, he mused. She had a tendency to drift in and out of his life. He never got used to it, though he was often of the same inclination. It was one reason his life consisted of processing eight hours each day and walking home alone to his quarters. His quarters. He couldn't even say for sure whether E had been to them since that day so long ago when she rescued him with her light, her curious cold radiance. Hers was a brilliant white light, not a warm yellow light. Also not the dull grey light never changing outside his windows. And not like the sunlight falling into the circle of trees on that day when *she* handed him that paper, the one with her "artwork" scrawled on it. But maybe like the silvery light shadows on the underside of the bridge across the river, yes, maybe like that. He wished so much to see it again. He felt so alone. Everyone he knew was gone. Many died around the time of the Change. Why he hadn't died was always a question in his mind. For what purpose had he been spared.

This purpose always felt obscured from him. He supposed it was this way with everyone, although others appeared from the outside to be surer than him. It was possible to blame it on suppression via the Adolescent Censor Program—his fragmented youth served to destroy any possibility of a future imbued with meaning. And there was the complication of his unintentional awareness of this fragmentation. Most were not aware of the redactions in their past. The cloaking process was meant to remain secret, from what he could surmise. To be tortured by one's fractured memories was not the goal of the Censor program. But these were not topics discussed openly, and so this theory had remained unconfirmed. Of course it's possible experiments were carried out on human subjects. The government was not above such actions, though it always hid them well.

She handed him the paper. He took it, warm and damp in his hand. He examined it. He traced her "artwork" with his finger and his face grew hot. The Censor was at the window. He sensed the red eyes behind him. He handed the paper back to her and walked away toward the narrow strip of trees beyond the eastern perimeter of the yard. She followed him. He knew what he was doing. The Censor's range did not extend beyond the confines of the yard. But no—he felt sure this was not what had actually happened. He did not know what he was doing, only that there were infinite versions of the scenario, creating and destroying in his mind every moment of every day. It didn't matter what he did in any of them, for the evidence was destroyed at day's end, ushering in his dread. *The smoke, the demons.*

An earlier attempt at exorcism had failed. He had seen the exorcist for a few months, but the treatments did not take hold. They were an odd group, the exorcists. They proliferated after the Change, like payday loan sharks circling in a depressed area of the city. There was no doubt that a small percentage of the populace had gone bat-shit crazy. And inevitably there are always those waiting to capitalize on others whose realities have fractured beyond easy repair.

Another fragment entered—he was back at university, in the classroom, sitting behind E and staring at the back of her head. The professor was speaking in a language he could not comprehend. E appeared to be listening, her head cocked, her grey eyes pointed to the front of the room. The light from the window glinted in the reddish tints of her dark hair. The light faded. He was thinking about the end of his life and how soon it might come. He was not afraid of dying; he was afraid of living. Platitudes such as this nauseated him, and yet he found in them some strange, cloying comfort. Now he stared at E's neck. He stared out the window. He stared at the blank paper his professor placed on his desk. There was no end to his staring.

10.

At the meta-meeting he was asked to report out on processing. There was not much to say. He read the numbers aloud in a dull voice. At the end, the managers murmured their approval and he returned to his machine atop the artificial wood grain. He took a can of compressed air from the shelf and blasted all the detritus out of his keyboard—a satisfying task. He reviewed the current status of requests and set to work: *click check-boxes, submit, approve, reply, reply all, attach file, ctrl-c, ctrl-v, confirm.*

He went to the coffeehouse and E was sitting there as if she had never left. She said nothing of her recent absence. He sometimes wondered if she were an agent. He'd heard rumors of shadowy operatives working for an underground program to repair damage caused by the Censors. It sounded far-fetched, but he could see her doing that kind of work. He didn't think she could conceal it from him, though. He felt he knew her too well.

Or at least he did at one time. He sipped his coffee and watched her talk to him, her lips moving around the words shunted from her brain.

In the tunnels this morning I saw our old professor, she said.

He coughed but said nothing. This seemed unlikely given they'd gone to university hundreds of miles from this city. Though perhaps the man had left that rural outpost like so many others did after the Change. Out there, supply delivery took weeks and self-sufficiency was not at all viable.

He could no longer even recall the professor's face in his mind. It was possible he had even passed the man in the tunnels before and not recognized him. No one in the tunnels had faces he recognized.

Are you even listening to me, she asked.

She stood up as if to leave, [readjust, recalculate, reestablish personal perimeter], but no, she was refilling her cup. He exhaled into his own empty cup, the bitter coffee fumes rising sharply. She returned to her seat, crossed and re-crossed her legs.

Did you speak to him, he asked.

Briefly. He asked about you. He wanted to know

why you never came back to his class after that day.

There was no simple answer to this question and she knew it. He stood up as if to leave, but only refilled his cup. He watched her from the coffee machine. An erect reed refusing to sway. He felt himself sinking.

He woke up on the floor, a ring of concerned faces peering down at him. E was next to him, his head in her lap. She offered him water. He took the cup and drank as the crowd dispersed. She helped him back to his seat.

Has that happened before?

He shook his head.

Did you feel faint?

Yes...I remember the color draining from everything until it was just grainy static, then waking up in your lap.

She fidgeted with her cup and looked away.

Perhaps too much coffee and not enough sleep.

Yes, perhaps.

He told his supervisor he was feeling unwell before returning to his quarters. He did not feel terrible. But something was wrong. It felt as if something was missing, but he had no idea what it was. In another time he watched a figure striding away down the sidewalk, smoke drifting upward, illuminated in the orange glow of the sodium street lamps. He felt an urge for a cigarette. He saw E walk away from the stone building. He saw clouds gather, recede; felt the sun fall upon him with suddenness. Rapid movements, woolen tights, a sodden piece of paper turning to pulp in his hand. The gaping quarry below. He awoke covered in sweat, the same dull light outside his opaque window, his mouth dry. *Down there, down there.*

11.

Far away someone related to him might still be alive. He had no idea. He carried a distance between himself and everyone else from childhood to the beginning of the end of his youth. Now was stasis. Now was parsed into processing, meeting E at the coffeehouse, the fragments of his mind spinning forever in spirals like an old-time color wheel pointed at an aluminum Christmas tree. How can a person lose so much and still be alive.

He got up and made a cup of coffee. The silence in the building clung to him, making him conscious of each tiny noise. Slight slurp from a sip of coffee. Clink of porcelain as he set the cup back in its saucer. Paper scratching as he turned a page in his book. He felt hyper-stimulated by the constant awareness of his own existence, the actions he took, the thoughts in his head. Nausea rose and he returned to the bedroom to lie down.

He woke with the tree in his mind, his hand reaching out, fingers pushing through the feathery moss to the deep slit where the glossy orange trunk split. Warmth pulsed from that spot. He stood alone in the strip of woods behind the house, looking out into the yard, staring at her small back as she walked away, down the gravel path next to the house. Walking, not running. His heart calm, not racing. He raised his face to the sky, reached out to steady himself against the smooth, warm wood. The ozone rushed up his nose—it was going to rain.

He fell back asleep and dreamed of the river, a snowy day spent traversing its banks, the watery brown-green now coated in white. The sun glittered on the powdery snow, whipped by the wind into tiny whirling dervishes. He stared at the unbroken white slopes, the light dazzling his vision so the white turned in places to pink and when he blinked dark sheets fell across his eyes. Her eyes, so grey, so immutable. She, standing there next to him, like the reeds now standing in the cold, frosted over yet still erect, swaying or perhaps not, his vision blurred as it was by the refracted light of the snow. The snow, spread like cake frosting to the very edge of the banks, melted slowly in the sun, dripping its purity into the brown water, cleansing out the heavy silt roiling in its currents. The river had never looked so clean to him. Like seeing her for the first time, after walking into the classroom. But no, she was not there, at the river, not then. There, she was, maybe in his mind, but not there, somewhere else.

When he awoke again he experienced his usual shock at the lack of change in light seen through the opaque window. He lay in bed for hours staring at the window, seeing its panes as snow-covered—not frosted to obscure the bleak landscape outside. The sorrow at having lost so many of his memories mingled with the ache he felt over this now barren place.

Now he sat in the coffeehouse waiting for E. Now his machine clattered on the artificial wood grain. Now he processed credits. Now he attended the meta-meeting. Now he walked the halls. Now he walked the tunnels. Now he rode the silent elevator in his building. He looked for faces but they were obscured, heads pointed down, eyes averted, sleeves of flesh wrapped around the glistening mechanisms of life. *Where has everyone gone?*

She stood next to him on the green grass. The air was still. From down the street he could hear children playing. Somewhere nearby a dog barked. He felt the weight of her expectancy as he felt the eyes of the Censor at his back. The subtlety of his life had not yet been ironed out. But no, it had been, in a way, by the Censor. Still, in the distance he could see a future. He did not know if it belonged to him. Her arm hovered in front of him, thin and brown, the tiny blond hairs excited to their full height. He looked away.

12.

E began smoking again. He considered it, too, but adoption of another vice might complicate his daily routines, a risk he was afraid to take. Routine would either save him or it would kill him, or perhaps both. What was the old adage...what doesn't kill us, saves us. Or what doesn't save us, kills us. It was probably unimportant. Maybe what cannot be exorcised saves us. He could at least hope for that.

He remembered he'd seen E at a party once, long after he'd dropped that class. It was an afterlife party, where everyone had died and passed into the waiting room beyond. He'd avoided most theme parties like this while at university, but his friend had dragged him along, having an interest in one of the attendees. E wore corpse paint and a black lace dress, high at the neck. Her hair was teased up into a dark halo around her white face. He noticed her immediately, though their eyes met only once during the evening. Dilated pupils loomed large in her grey eyes. He thought she must be on something. Still, the intensity of her stare remained the same as it did that day he had opened the classroom door, her head turning, his life sliding down.

Again he saw himself standing in the yard. Take this, she said. But no, she hadn't spoken. The gesture implied the statement. There was no one else around, at least not in the immediate vicinity. But the Censor was around. The Censor was always around. Noise of others not far away trickled into the horseshoe-shaped yard, flat as it was with its steep, sloping earthen sides, like an unwashed mixing bowl. Had she come out of the woods? It was possible to walk from her house, two houses down, through the swath of woods, to his yard, without anyone seeing. Had she meant to be secretive? Yes, it seemed likely she had come out of the woods, given the orientation of her body to his in that moment. Her small delicate frame in the shadow of his tall narrow frame. The excitement bright in her eyes. He could see it now. She reached into the tight pocket of her cut-offs.

He came to on the floor of his office, staring at the artificial wood grain from below. The patterns looked surprisingly organic. His eyes edged to the door, but no one stood watching. He scrambled to his feet and eased himself back into the chair, took a sip of water. He felt feverish and light-headed; mild palpitations throbbed in his chest. The idea of leaving early again presented itself, but it could mean arousing the suspicion of his supervisor. He forced his mind back into normal routine. Normal. *Reply, forward, attach, reply, approve, click submit, confirm, ctrl-c, ctrl-v, connection drop.* Several hours passed. *The smoke, the demons.* The tunnels, his quarters.

He entered the classroom on that first day back at university. Tall windows lined the opposite side of the room from where they sat, one behind the other. Sun streamed in through the dust motes floating in the ether, a drowsy pleasure seeping through his body. He stared at the back of her head, her hair gathered and wound into a tight bun. She tilted her head to the right with her chin pushed forward, her eyes focused on the professor at the front of the room. He could not understand what the professor was saying. He rubbed his eyes, the restless drowsiness moving around inside him, refusing departure.

13.

He ascended from the tunnels to the coffeehouse. E sat at their usual table with her legs crossed and a cup of coffee steaming in front of her. He tried to take a picture of the scene with his mind before she noticed him. He thought about how there would no longer ever be a time when he saw the sunlight filtered through her hair like on that day in the classroom. He swiped his card and filled his cup at the machine. She caught his eye and smiled. Maybe it looked a little forced but he no longer knew her face well enough. When he sat down her smile was gone.

Do you want to talk about the river?

The river...

She stared at him. Yes, the river. Do you remember what happened at the river?

It felt like the light had shifted—a literal impossibility.

I don't...the river...why now.

She sighed. Crossed and re-crossed her legs, sipped from her cup. He thought she was about to leave. Sudden fear seized him. He stood and muttered goodbye, walked quickly to the door.

Back at his desk he stared unseeing at the twin screens. The tree with the orange bark rose from the soil of his mind. He yearned to run his hand over its smooth curves, spiraling to its mossy center at the fork. Nothing else seemed so important. But like always it remained out of reach. The grainy static returned, creeping across his line of sight to obscure the tree's image. He felt himself slipping through a shadowy passage. *Down there, down there.*

INTERLUDE

I remember it was late on a summer afternoon. I was sitting in the back yard near the edge—where the lawn drops off into the patch of woods between our houses on this street and their houses on that street. Mother had called for me to come in for supper but I love this time of day—the in-between time when the sun is still shining but lower in the sky. I always want to hold it close, the yellow light transfusing everything, the shadows growing faster and wider, darkening the corners and lengthening the lines to infinity.

As I sit there staring at the indigo shadows twisting around the trees, I see movement in the woods way down on the path. It's a girl. As she comes into view I recognize her as one who lives on that street. I don't know her but I've seen her around. She is small but a little older than me, I think. She is moving with purpose and I can almost feel the blood rushing beneath her skin as she hurries up the hill.

All of a sudden she stops. She is at the tree, the one with the orange bark. There are all kinds of rumors about that tree. About what's hidden in it, about how it has some secret power. Sometimes I see boys down there, reaching inside the hollow where the trunk splits into two limbs. Mother doesn't let me go in the woods, though. She doesn't like me mixing with the kids from that street, and they are the ones always messing around in the woods. They also cut through our yard to get to their street and Mother doesn't like that, either. But there isn't much she can do. She is at work when they do it on their way home from school.

The girl stands there for a while with her hand on the tree. Then she continues walking until she is at the yard directly behind mine. I peer through the trees and I can see the boy who lives at that house. He is standing in the yard facing the back of his house. I don't know this boy too much, either. But one time I was in the yard and he came down the path, cutting through our yard. He looked surprised to see me. *Hello*, he said. I said hi back, even though I knew Mother wouldn't want me talking to him. He didn't say anything else, just kept walking. His face looked sad.

Now the girl is at the edge of the yard. She starts walking across the lawn toward the boy. I see his head turn toward her. I can't hear if she called to him or not. She walks right up to him and pulls something out of her pocket. They stand there close together for a minute or two. She holds out whatever it is but I can't see what happens, if he takes it or not, because of the way they are both standing with their backs to me. I see his head turn quick to look up at the window. They move apart and she walks away, down the path next to his house. The boy runs up onto the deck and goes inside the house. Soon Mother calls again and I go inside too.

PART II

1.

In the middle of a sentence, the professor had begun speaking in an arcane dialect she recalled her parents using when she was a child. Up to that moment she had been thinking about the river, of its soft green banks and chocolate brown currents. The professor was staring at her as he talked about a time of natural violence, when the rivers would dry up, the grass burn to cinders. He warned of what would come later—how once enclosed, people would retreat to their dreams. She cocked her head to the right. She felt him behind her. She knew he was staring at the sunlight, the motes floating in the yellow haze. But this was not about him, not now. She listened to the professor say there would be some who could reach these day-sleepers in their dreams, and how crucial their role would be in treating the condition.

Up here, up here, in the center of synaptic activity, when so many others stare down with a fog in their heads.

What she saw center-tangled was a bundle of neural pathways, sparking with activity. This, this was just a leg, she'd said. His face a jigsaw puzzle of confusion at her interpretation. Her center crisscrossed with nerve fibers, her cares concerned with axons and dendrites. These other acts occurred outside her sphere, encouraged only by the one who was standing apart from her.

What the other did was of no concern to her. She thought she was choosing to ignore, but it may have been involuntary—this dismissal of shared urgency. She thought her mind remained pure, that nothing had been redacted. But this was unconfirmed.

Before the Change she had walked the streets in the evenings. She remembered one night the orange glow of the street lamps illuminating her steady path along the still snow-covered sidewalks. She walked north, staring straight ahead, crossed the east-west street, continued north up the same side, crossed over to the opposite side, soon crossed back, and returned south by the same route. Her choice of location for reversal in direction would have seemed arbitrary to an observer, yet the boldness of its execution indicated otherwise. The night was cold, with a bitter wind, not a night many would choose for a stroll, unless perhaps a fire was in one's head. But her pace did not betray heat, so measured was it. So measured it was and yet lacking in any destination of obvious distinction. It was true she was dressed warmly, suggesting predetermination. A hat covered her head and she wore a heavy coat, though not of any great length, for visible below its hem were woolen tights covering her legs. She moved with swift, even motion, as if in a rush, and yet a rush to get where. To get there, and yet there was nowhere, to an observer's eye. A glimpse at profile, from a point several meters to the immediate west, yielded the features of an aquiline nose and a set jaw, the latter betraying further evidence of explicit intent. The heels of her boots struck the concrete in staccato rhythm, fading out as she moved further south, a sudden sound of certainty struggling to be heard.

2.

She arranged for them to begin meeting at the coffee-house. It had been so long, she wasn't even sure if he remembered, or if he did, what he remembered. Her mind a knife's edge, his a shattered mirror. These days now, since university, like another world; no, not just like, it was a different world. It had not been so hard for her to adjust; she had it easier than others. Her mind whole, unclouded, her sense of the rational an asset in a time when making sense of everything was a challenge most could not face. There was too much newness—this present life had burst forth from its chrysalis in an instant, shedding its warm lining to now cold-glisten in the perpetual dull grey light. Yes, there was something in this new life that fit well to her psyche.

Now he sits before her, cup in hand, a broken vessel puzzling over how to fit its own shards back together. She is not sure how to handle him. Gentle probing at his mind yields little insight into what is now housed within. It could, in fact, hold secrets of hers; though in his state he is unlikely to even realize this. It seems what information is available to him comes without warning, and with no context. This is part conjecture, for he still shares little with her. And so they sit, week after week, drinking coffee and failing each other in their own separate ways.

She wonders where his mind is, where it goes, where it has been before her, after her, with her. Those days of him sitting behind her, his breath on the nape of her neck. What happened at the river. The rope of time stretched between them, alternately picked up and dropped by one or the other. He gets up from the table now, she thinks he is going to refill his cup, but too late to call out, she sees him disappear into the tunnels.

She returns to her quarters. Troubled by a recent dream-filming session, she stretches her long limbs out on the wood floor to ease their quaking. She'd been shocked to find one of her own dreams playing inside another person's mind, a dream she's had since childhood, a dream of a tree with orange bark, standing in a narrow strip of woods between two rows of houses.

The dreamer is a woman named F of indeterminate age, small and fine-boned, skin supple and unmarred by wrinkles, yet she does not seem young. She too is an artist, an illustrator, who has experienced vivid dreams since the Change. In an effort to understand them, she began to draw and paint what she saw. She hangs this artwork on the walls in her studio. On her first visit E felt a familiar panic consume her when she saw the paintings.

E dreams of the tree almost every night. Sometimes she sees the tree, standing before her or at the periphery of her vision. Other times she is the tree—her arms the limbs and her legs the long forked trunk—rooted far in the earth. When she is the tree she feels a power she has never felt before—a strength of spirit she did not think to be possible in human form. It throbs inside her center. Up here and down there merge into one, like never in waking life.

3.

She walks the tunnels for entire afternoons. Wearing her wool coat she descends from the lobby of her building to the depths, where she follows predetermined circuits, sketched out on thin graph paper for weeks in advance. It is not so much a pastime as a compulsion. Sometimes she deviates from her course to follow a certain individual. Once she had seen him, returning to his quarters after work, hunched over hurrying with rigid steps. She watched as his fear filled the tunnel, causing all others within it to move faster, hastening with sudden desperation. Drawn to his fear, she followed, entering his building and shadowing him all the way to his floor.

Long ago she had visited him there, in his quarters. It was soon after the Change and she had sensed he needed her. When she arrived he was in trouble. He had not been following the new protocol establishing artificial circadian rhythms. She'd been angry with him that day, and had left as soon as he was stable. She saw his refusal to adapt as weakness, his stubborn reaction a mask for passivity, something she could not tolerate. Yet over time her feelings lost their brittleness as she came to understand how broken his mind really is. She doesn't know what the Censors did to him, but she thinks it was not supposed to be this way. She knows of no other case so extreme, although she wonders about F and her dreams.

Now she sees him in the coffeehouse and feels helpless. They had both disappeared, at different times and in their own ways. Often it feels as if there is nothing tying them together anymore, if indeed there ever had been. He fascinates her but this fascination is of clinical detachment.

The river, the river—she wants to talk to him about the river but she is afraid. Afraid of what it might do to him. His reluctance to go there in his mind erupts before her every day. Her reluctance to leave it alone is like slow poison in her veins. *Up here, up here,* where it all makes sense, where there is not the flushed flurry she cannot control. It was the other one that day at the river, the one standing near her, behind her, *apart from her.* The last time she sensed its presence drawing close to an eclipse, perhaps the only true time.

She goes to see F and leaves in disarray. F's mind frightens her, the lurid details of her dreams, she does not see how this person who is so quiet, so delicate and gentle on the outside, how her mind can contain such frightening imagery. And the paintings on the walls, how does F live with those around her at all times. After leaving, E does word problems in her head for hours to restore the order displaced by F's dream-chaos. Still, she cannot stop thinking about the tree and its presence in both their dreams.

4.

She meets him at the coffeehouse. She worries now that he has passed out twice. But his sensitivity makes her hesitant to talk too much about it. About the dreams and what is happening to him. Why he cannot seem to keep it together.

How is your vitamin D level, she asks.

Fine.

Nothing more. He is withdrawn as usual. Not in a sullen way. More like it is impossible for him to reach outside of himself. Like there is no key to unlock him and he knows it, so he sits there trapped, looking out in this helpless state. He gets up, she thinks just to fill his cup, but instead she sees him walk toward the door and he is gone.

That night she sits in her quarters making illicit incense. Since the fragrance sickness epidemic swept through the enclosed cities, all scented products had

been banned, even those made from natural ingredi-
ents. But she cannot survive without her scents. She
procures the herbs and resins on the black market—
a loose network of indoor growers, processors, and sellers
without whom she would be lost. She will bring some of
the scents she creates to him with the hope it will ease
his ragged mind, help restore to him what has been lost.

Now she prepares for sleep, following the herbal
protocols necessary to prevent her from lingering too
long in her dreams. She thinks of him, knowing he is
more than likely not following such protocols, despite
her urging him to do so. It is so hard, this watching
another person unravel when one feels there could be a
way to prevent and even help reverse the process, if only
the other person could participate. But the barriers in
his mind persist.

5.

Dreaming now, E stands on the shore of the river, a torrent of brown silty liquid rushing past a few feet away from her boots. He stands to her left, staring up at the underside of the bridge. He is always there, and yet only ever present that one day. Many afternoons they have spent walking the path parallel to the river. She feels him next to her, but she doesn't know what he feels. He is so quiet; she often wonders if he is there at all.

On the university grounds they also used to walk, after the class with the professor who spoke of a horrific future, the one who had led her to what she would one day become. It was before he had left that class, before his presence in the seat behind her disappeared. So many walks they had taken, and it was mostly she who had talked. He listened, always attentive, occasionally asking brief questions, wanting clarification on this or that point she was making. He was good at that. He was so good, in fact, it had never occurred to her how little he told her about himself. Later she considered if she had been self-centered, if the reason he had said so little was because he'd simply been waiting for her to ask him questions of her own.

After so many years, she still doesn't know how to get through to him. He is as reticent as he used to be, perhaps even more so. Even asking questions leads to evasive actions on his part. So perhaps this was never the right way to go about it. Maybe if she'd asked him questions back then it wouldn't have mattered. What she wishes she could do is read his dreams. She feels sure this would finally unlock his mind to her. But she cannot do it on her own. He needs to come to her. He needs to want to tell her, to open himself to her, or else she will never find anything of substance to restore.

6.

The next week she travels to another city to record a regular client's dreams. She does not like traveling to the other cities. They all seem the same, which depresses her. But there are only so many people who can afford to have their dreams filmed. Her clients are scattered throughout the region, which means she is away often. Whenever she is somewhere else she worries about him. She knows he must wonder where she is but she cannot tell him what she does to earn credits. The equipment she uses is illegal and she can't risk putting him in danger by letting him in on this aspect of her life. So she compartmentalizes, as she knows he too does with her. It's perhaps one of the ways they fail each other, although she's not certain. Sometimes she thinks it's better this way—to only know certain parts of another. Besides, most days she does not feel complete, and so she does not even have the whole of herself to give.

After filming the dreams she spends time talking with her clients. She asks about their sleeping habits, how often they dream, what they feel about their dreams. If they are open to it, she advises them on the herbal preparations used to limit how long they dream. She takes notes during these sessions and studies them. She is still learning what she has to offer these people. The professor helps her but it's not easy. It's not a skill one picks up overnight. One must learn the nuances and limits of one's gift only through experience. It can take years. But the professor thinks she shows promise. For now she does what she can and her clients are grateful in return.

7.

She visits F again at her quarters. This client worries her, but she keeps paying and E can't afford to refuse. The woman looks gaunt with dark circles under her eyes. Her hair has lost its luster and her movements are listless. She lies down on the bed and E administers the sleep tonic. Soon F's eyelids are flickering and E begins to film. The dream begins with a scene of a girl rushing out of a house. A woman's voice is heard yelling after her. The girl runs to a strip of woods adjacent to the backyard of the house. The perspective shifts, allowing E to see what the girl is seeing. The overgrown brambles of midsummer, thorns scratching the skin of her thighs as she hurries up the hill through the woods. She trips over a rock, catches herself before falling, continues on. Suddenly the tree with orange bark is in front of her. The tallest tree in this scraggly patch of suburban woods, its massive trunk split into two main limbs reaching toward the sky. The girl approaches the tree, places her hand at the hollow of the fork. She closes her eyes as she moves her hand through the soft moss growing there. Sunlight falls through the trees onto her thin arms as she stands close to the tree. After a moment she continues on through the woods, slower now as she approaches another yard. Through the hanging leaves she sees a boy standing behind the house. His head turns toward her as she slips out of the woods. But then, as if he's heard something, he looks back at the house. The girl reaches into her pocket as she continues walking slowly across the yard. The background fades.

F wakes, her pupils dilated in fear. E offers her a glass of water.

Do you remember the dream? she asks.

I remember the tree, the orange one...and a boy.

E takes a few notes. Did you recognize the boy?

No, I don't think so. It's hard, though...I only saw his face so briefly.

E places her hand on the woman's shoulder. I know it's hard to remember, but it's important. Is there anything familiar about these surroundings?

F nods. The house at the beginning, I think this is where I lived for a few years as a child.

E smiles at her. That's good. There's just one more thing I want to ask you about before I go. When you woke up, you looked afraid, but in the dream I didn't sense fear from you. Do you know what scared you?

F sits up and rubs her eyes. I'm not sure. It was just a sensation, almost as if I had been doing something forbidden.

E nods absently before rising to leave.

Wait, F says. What do you think it means?

I don't know yet. I'm not an expert. Maybe it's just a memory fragment. But you should rest. I'll see myself out.

8.

At the coffeehouse today she's pleased to find him more talkative.

You seem in better spirits, she says.

Yes. I've been taking my vitamin D injections more regularly, and I'm using the sun lamp you brought me a long time ago.

She remembers again the state in which she'd found him on that day and the frustration she'd felt with his passive resistance to the new routines.

Well, I'm glad you've been taking better care of yourself at least. And how is work going?

He rolls his eyes. Oh please. I know you don't like to hear about it.

She smiles. Maybe tell me something about one of your colleagues, instead of boring talk about processing credits.

He laughs. Okay, well, let's see...two more managers

gave themselves raises and new offices. Yesterday my supervisor stopped by to complain about this no less than 15 times. And I've received five invitations for office baby showers in the last week. Apparently no one has noticed the world suffered an ecological collapse due in part to overpopulation.

She laughs. It is so rare to see him like this—she wishes they could talk longer, but he must return to work.

Before he leaves she gives him the incense. He seems pleased. With eyes closed, he passes one of the sticks beneath his nose and breathes in.

Mmm...cedarwood. How did you know?

She smiles. Make sure you turn the vent on in your quarters when you burn it. Even a trace of it noticed in the hallway could get you fined.

I have serious doubts about whether anyone else even lives in my building. But thank you, I will be careful.

They part ways and she walks the tunnels for several hours. The tunnels fascinate her, how the populace moves within these grimy interstices between the places they want and need to be. As in-between zones they are perfect for studying the truth in people's expressions, to find evidence of the anxieties and desires they so often mask when above ground. She often sketches what she's observed in these faces and later paints portraits based on the drawings. Stacks of these paintings fill a small room in her quarters. No one has ever seen them. This saddens her if she dwells on it for too long. Though she is not one to often pine for the past, she sometimes misses the nervous excitement of showing her art in galleries. But people's interest in art waned after the Change, when life became so much more utilitarian in nature. People wanted nothing but to shut their minds down in their off hours—to halt the mad parade of thoughts—and so what now passes for entertainment comes almost always from a screen.

9.

F is not doing well. E visits her and finds the woman even gaunter, as if she is physically shrinking. Her cheeks are hollow and her dull hair now appears to be losing its color. Her voice is so soft E can hardly understand the words she speaks. She is feverish and raves about the boy in the dream, saying he did no wrong but she fears she may have caused him trouble. *The Censor at the window,* she mutters. A brief, almost lucid diatribe follows about the tree with orange bark in the woods behind his house, about how the tree cursed them all as children, doomed them to a stunted existence. All of this arrives in short bursts between dry gasps for breath. E is concerned. She doesn't know what to do for the woman. She gets her to drink some water and cautions her to stay in bed while the fever lasts. But at the suggestion of a doctor, F shakes her head with vigor. No doctor, no doctor, she whispers.

E contacts the professor but he has little advice to share.

It sounds as if she is in the latter stages of the condition, he says.

What will happen to her?

We don't really know. There are stories of people literally disintegrating as they are wholly subsumed into dream life. I'm not sure I believe that, but even if a body remains behind we have no way of knowing the truth of what has happened.

E thanks him and returns to F's bedside. She does what she can to make the woman comfortable before saying goodbye. F no longer seems lucid and E feels a brief compulsion to stay with her through the night. But that feeling passes and in its place an instinct to leave arrives. She senses she has done all she can and now she must not interfere in the natural course of events.

10.

E returns to her quarters, worried about F but also thinking of the tree, of the girl and the boy in the dream. It feels familiar, like a memory. In her distracted state she neglects to take her usual herbal preparation. She soon falls asleep and enters a green world where sunlight streams down through the tree canopy to the dry leaf litter below. She slips into F's body, feeling her own melt away, as up here and down there join into one. The girl's lithe brown limbs now belong to her as she runs through the strip of woods behind the houses, the thorns tearing the skin of her thighs, leaving red lines jagged across the flesh. She feels not pain but exhilaration. Reaching the tree she stops and bows her head. She reaches out toward the cleft where the trunk splits. She slides her small hand along the smooth bark, her fingers tingling as they reach the mossy fringe surrounding the cleft. She rests her hand in the cool hollow and feels the warm sun on her bare arms and legs. Leaving the tree now she walks to the edge of the yard, his yard.

She wakes up and starts to paint with urgency. It is a new painting, based on a drawing she found in an old textbook she bought during her last trip to the other cities. She layers the paint in thick textures, lengthening the lines and darkening the centers. She feels a quickening of her pulse as her brush moves across the canvas. In her mind she sees herself approaching her other. She is nearer to it than ever before. The eclipse is almost complete. When the painting is done, she immediately hangs it on the wall. As she gazes at it other scenes take shape in her mind, the beginnings of other paintings yet to come.

INTERLUDE

I remember standing in the back yard after a bad session with the Censor. I felt numb inside and my head was pulsing. Being outside helped despite the hot, still air. I didn't know how much more I could take of the Censor. The redactions were making it hard to study for school, even though they were supposed to be targeted to specific thoughts. It felt like something was wrong, a malfunction perhaps. I couldn't believe it was supposed to feel this way.

As I'm standing there I know the Censor is watching from the window. I avoid looking up. I want it to think I'm not afraid, that I don't live every moment of every day in fear and worry over the thoughts I'm having. But this is hard because it means I have to act, and I'm not a good actor. So I stand there and stare into space, a habit I've picked up along the way. I stare into space and think about nothing.

Suddenly I hear a noise behind me—the snap of a twig breaking. I turn and I see her, this girl walking out of the strip of woods behind our houses. She lives down the street, a couple of houses away. Of course we know each other in the way all kids growing up on a street together know each other. But I've never paid her much mind. She's younger than me, the type always hanging around the older kids trying to be noticed.

I steal a quick glance at the window and see the red glare of the Censor's eyes. Panic rises. I turn back to the girl. She's walking toward me on the lawn, the green grass electrified in the yellow light. She gets close, looks up at me as she pulls a piece of paper out of the pocket of her jean shorts. She's smiling as she holds it out for me to see. I take it and examine it. It's a series of pencil drawings. It looks like she's traced them from somewhere but made her own modifications. My head begins to ache as I feel myself heating up inside. I can't think about this now. The Censor is watching. I feel it reaching out toward my mind through the window glass and across the yard to where I'm standing, holding the paper, staring at it with sore eyes.

I tell the girl she needs to go. I fold up the paper and give it back to her. She looks hurt. I can't do anything about that now. My head feels like a clanging bell. The girl walks away down the path next to the house. I stand there for a moment, trying to concentrate on nothing, to clear my head of the imagery already taking shape there. But I know it's too late. I turn and climb the stairs to the deck. I go inside.

PART III

1.

In here, in here, where it all began, and where it all will end. Sitting at his desk, he stares with clarity at the twin screens. He is back at work after medical leave. His boss had walked in, found him blacked out on the floor. He had protested, couldn't stand the thought of a week confined to his quarters. But there was protocol to follow. He was considered a security risk. Someone could walk into his office while he was unconscious and download credits from his machine. It would only take seconds. He had no choice but to acquiesce.

Now his fingers clatter across the keyboard, the machine thrumming on the artificial wood grain. He will not pass out this time, of that he feels certain. This is a new feeling: a disconnection from desire, a midpoint of focus from which there feels like no return. His mind is clear. He stretches out his fingers under the lamp, his skin almost translucent, like that of everyone else in this sunless world.

His colleague is on extended leave and so he must do everything now. But it is not so much. It's still the slow time of year, when people slip into hibernation and requests drop to a minimum. Last week he even had time to stabilize his machine so it no longer clatters on the desk. It's as if he's inherited his breathing rights all at once, despite the artificial air.

He takes a break and walks to the coffeehouse. There he finds E sitting calmly, as if she's always been there. Maybe she has. He's never been to her quarters. He has seen her leave the coffeehouse, though. He doesn't know where she goes, what she does. She does not share this information with him, although he's also never asked.

She looks up at him and smiles.

He nods and sits, sips at his coffee.

How are you feeling, she asks.

Alive and awake.

That much I can see.

It's all I can see, too.

Will you ever step into the light again? Like that day by the river.

The river flows through his mind, cold and clear. He sees himself with her, kneeling in the snow, marveling at how the water is no longer brown. They can see the riverbed now, scattered with smooth stones.

Some days are meant to stand alone, he says. The distance keeps it in place.

But why. What do you mean?

That's how it's always been. The light is gone. The distance remains.

I might not always be here, you know.

Meaning what?

I mean this dialogue we're having—you don't take much advantage of it. So will you be prepared for when it disappears?

He used to ask her questions, long ago, before the Change. On days by the river, or walking near the pond at the university. She talked and he listened. She told him about her childhood, about the tree in the woods behind her house. There was something hidden in it, she said. What was it, he had asked. But she didn't know. She had just heard rumors and once, while sitting quietly as dusk fell at the edge of her back yard, where the lawn turned to brambles and the woods began, she had seen figures near the tree, engaged in furtive motion. He had gone quiet then and she'd asked him what was wrong.

But he couldn't say. He didn't know what was wrong, only felt an uneasiness push through his mind, clouding his thoughts.

2.

Despite the newfound clarity in his mind, gaps still yawn wide between ridges of uncertainty: the redactions. Although he isn't always sure what was redacted and what has disappeared through the organic process of memory loss, helped along as it has been by illicit substances consumed over time. He wants to blame the Censor for all he has lost, but he's afraid this isn't true.

He drifts in and out of sleep at his desk, processing requests in between these micro-naps. The halls remain empty, which is just as well. He eschews most contact with his colleagues for their chatter does not register with him. It revolves around self-curation, new places to spend credits, and people known only through screens. It sounds alien to him. But he does not feel ill will toward his colleagues, only mystification at their interests and concerns. After so long their familiarity has grown to resemble comfort, and as such they feel necessary to his existence in a nebulous way he cannot ever clarify to himself.

Where have you been, E asks when he arrives at the coffeehouse.

The meta-meeting ran late.

She laughs. Sounds painful.

He nods, sips at his coffee. They sit in silence. The others move around, entering from the tunnels, purchasing coffee, drinking coffee, returning to the tunnels. He looks out the window where nothing ever changes. He looks at E. She is reading now.

What's the book?

She holds it up. *A Primer on Dream Interpretation.*

As if thus summoned, his dream from the night before rises from the murk of his mind. He'd only been able to recall impressions when he wrote in the dream book that morning. But now it all rushes in on him. Community members hurrying up a hill for a crucial gathering—a meeting to announce a decision. Whispers around him, worried faces. Are they speaking about him? He isn't sure. He did not feel a sense of menace so much as a powerful joined concern, rooted in all of these people together.

He wonders if she will ask him again about the river. He questions what value there could be in revisiting it with her. Maybe if they'd talked about it long ago it would have helped. But now it haunts his mind as a stabbing reminder of how life was not always this way, of how once he'd had a chance at living an unsplintered existence. Instead he asks her about the Censors.

What about them?

Anything you might know.

She cocks her head and stares at him. Why the sudden interest?

He begins to wish he hadn't brought it up. It's a project for work, he says. A literature review I'm conducting for a manager. I thought maybe you'd have some ideas for terms I could add to my search strategy.

He senses she doesn't believe him, but she starts to talk. He is disappointed in what she has to share. Nothing new, only the usual information everyone knows. He can't believe he once wondered if she were an agent.

3.

After work he descends to the tunnels feeling such despair he can barely walk. The end-of-day dread never stays away for long. It used to be the fading afternoon light of the winter months ushered in the dread. In a way he misses this, for now it rises every day without warning before him—a tall dark column just a hair's width from his face. After all these years it still shocks him. Just when he begins to experience what he assumes is "normal," this feeling is stripped from him.

He arrives at his building and climbs the ladder with effort. He drags his cinder block feet across the marble floor. But, wait, what is this? Another tenant is in the mail room. He forces his sluggish feet forward at a faster pace and enters the tiny alcove. Immediately he goes to his mailbox so as not to frighten off his neighbor. As he flips through the circulars, he peers from the corner of his eye at the person to his right, a man of average height wearing a grey suit and a fedora. Suddenly the man turns and smiles, holding up his bundle of mail.

Nothing but circulars!

He smiles back. Same here.

Have you lived here long? the man asks.

Ten years. And you're the first person I've ever seen in here.

The man raises his eyebrows. I find that hard to believe.

Well, it's true. How long have you been here?

The man begins edging toward the door. Just moved in, he calls over his shoulder as he leaves the room.

Wait! he yells, rushing out into the lobby.

But the man is gone, leaving only the usual silence.

He watches the floor numbers light up above the elevator. They rise all the way to the 15th floor. He has never been on the top floor. The elevator returns to the lobby and he steps into it. He pushes the 15 button and travels skyward. But the elevator stops at the 14th floor and refuses to go further. He gets out and enters the emergency stairwell where he finds a door to the stairs leading up to the 15th floor. But the door is more like a wall, with no handle or window. He places his hand on it and feels nothing.

He returns to his quarters and lies down on the bed. He stares at the window where the light never changes. He thinks about the man in the fedora, tries to picture him in his mind. Something is not right about him. He seems familiar but in a menacing way. And his outfit was strange. An outdated look. No one dresses like that anymore except for a costume party.

He checks his vitamin D and finds it low so he injects himself. Suddenly it feels unbearable to be in his quarters. He leaves and descends into the tunnels. The scene has not played in his mind for weeks now. He feels different, more stable in certain ways, though still subject to crashes like earlier. The end-of-day dread. He managed to stave it off this time. Perhaps it was the vitamin D; he resolves to start checking it regularly at day's end, instead of only in the morning.

With no destination in mind he wanders the tunnels for hours. At one point he thinks he sees E, hurrying along a little-used corridor near City Hall. But he can't be sure, and his attempts to follow her are thwarted by a large rat hissing at him, blocking his way forward. Few people are out at this hour on a weeknight. It would likely be pleasant to walk if the surroundings weren't a network of dark, clammy tunnels. But, as it is, the usual claustrophobia clings to him. The dripping of the condensation on the walls, the strange creaking and groaning noises, it all grows louder in his ears until he cannot stand it and returns to his building.

4.

At the coffeehouse the next day, he doesn't mention to E his trip through the tunnels. Instead he describes the man with the fedora to her.

That sounds like our old professor, she says.

He thinks back to the classroom, finds the man's face in the scraps of his remaining memory.

Of course. Yes, yes, you're right. It was definitely him.

She smiles. I told you I saw him recently but you didn't believe me.

He stands up.

Don't leave, she says.

He laughs. I'm just going to fill my cup.

When he returns he apologizes for not believing her.

It just didn't seem to make sense that he would be here, in the city. It still doesn't. And why in my building now. He said he just moved in. Do you think he's watching me?

She raises her eyebrows. Why would he be watching you? Do you have something to hide? And who do you think he is, anyway. He's just our old professor, right?

He frowns, uncertain of how much to say. Maybe. I'm probably just being paranoid. I haven't been sleeping well and my vitamin D is low.

Well, you're just a mess, aren't you. Why can't you ever keep up with the basics?

He stares into his cup. I don't know.

5.

The end-of-day dread transforms into the start-of-day dread. Or it is both. It's all mingled together is what it is, this torpor spreading through his body. He hasn't left his quarters since last seeing E at the coffeehouse. Now he rarely even leaves the bed. It took all of his strength to notify his supervisor of a need to take leave. E stops by after a few days. He lets her in but lies back down on the bed and turns toward the wall.

You need to get out of here, she says.

I can't. It's not that simple. Why can't you understand that.

She places her hand on his back but he shrinks further against the wall. She sighs and stands up.

I'm leaving, but I'll be back to check on you.

Two days later in the evening there is a knock on the door. He drags himself from the bed and looks through the peephole, expecting to find E. But it's not her. It's the man with the fedora, their old professor. He opens the door a couple of inches.

Can I help you?

The man stares at him, a look of concern on his face.

Are you ill? You look ill.

He shuts the door and leans against it, panic rising through his chest. The man knocks again.

Hello? Please open the door. This is important. You look ill. I can help you.

He quietly slides the deadbolt into place and backs away from the door.

In the kitchen he makes a cup of chamomile tea and sits at the table. Sound is increasing in intensity again. The clink of the tea cup against the saucer. The artificial birds singing their tuneless songs. The scrape of the chair legs against the tile floor. He returns to the bedroom and lies down, staring at the window, the never-changing light. He wishes for sleep to visit him but as long as he thinks of it he knows it will stay away.

He struggles out of bed the next morning and prepares to return to work. The HVAC system in the building is malfunctioning. Cold air blasts from the vents. He shivers in his lightweight sleeping garment as he waits for the bathtub to fill. Suddenly he is there again, in the bowl-shaped yard. The sun streams down through the trees. She walks toward him, across the green grass. He looks toward the window, sees the red eyes. He turns back toward her. She extends her small brown hand, a slip of paper held between her delicate fingers.

He comes to on the cold tile. Dull pain throbs in his head. He crawls to the tub, slides his tall frame into the hot water. The steam circles his head, easing the pain. He forces himself to think about that day, about her and what she showed him. But there is nothing but the same fragments, thin and brittle, about to crumble as he approaches them once more.

6.

Sitting at his desk now, filling requests. *Ctrl-c, ctrl-v, click check-box, approve, confirm.* Machine rattling again on the artificial wood grain. The tree with the orange bark rises in his consciousness, filling his veins with adrenalin, like auxins coursing through phloem. He sees her walking through the strip of woods. Chills raise the pale hairs on his arms. He feels nauseous. He looks down at the wood grain. Its symmetry draws his attention away from his roiling stomach. He reaches out and traces the grain with his near-translucent finger. Cool air blows down on him from the ceiling vent. Everywhere the HVAC systems are failing. In the hallways his colleagues whisper of an energy shortage at Central Control. He closes the door and switches on the portable heater at his feet. Fitting the earphones into the spaces where they go, he clicks on *Desire in Uneasiness* and returns to his work.

At the coffeehouse he considers whether to tell E about the professor's visit to his quarters. The man had acted strangely and it bothered him. But maybe it was best not to tell her. She'd acted surprised when he thought it strange for the man to suddenly appear in his building. He couldn't understand why she wouldn't think so.

What are you thinking about, she asks.

Nothing.

After finishing his coffee he gets up and walks to the tunnels.

Goodbye, she calls to him.

That evening in the lobby of his building he finds the professor waiting for the elevator. Oh, I'm glad to see you, the professor says.

Why is that.

The professor smiles. How are you feeling? I've been worried about you.

I'm better, thanks. You said you could help me. What did you mean—help me how?

The elevator door opens but neither of them moves.

Perhaps we could talk briefly at your quarters, the professor says.

Reluctantly he agrees and they enter the elevator. At his quarters he makes tea and they sit in the small anteroom.

So you've been passing out lately, the professor says.

What—wait, how do you know about that?

You have been, though, yes? What do you feel when you pass out?

I don't know. A certain dullness, I guess. It's hard to remember. But tell me how you know this. Only E was there that one time.

She's also here to help you. She has always tried to help you. Have you not noticed that? And yet you still resist her. Now, tell me what else do you feel when you lose consciousness. Do you see static? Do you remember...things?

What things?

Symbols. Recurring motifs or talismans. Some trigger or anchor that ties these experiences together.

I don't know what you're talking about.

You must try harder to understand. Do you remember my class?

Yes, some of it. But that was a long time ago.

Why did you leave—do you remember?

I couldn't understand you. I kept trying, but it was as if you were speaking in another language.

The professor nods absently.

Well, were you speaking another language or not?

In a way, yes. Because you were asleep, or rather at the edge of sleep, near enough to waking life to hear me, but not close enough to understand what I was saying.

That sounds absurd. Besides, I don't recall sleeping in your class.

The professor shakes his head. I said you were at the edge! Pay attention. The Change had not yet happened, but there were signs already. It's a reaction. Since then you've been drifting in and out, like so many others. Some can no longer even tell when they're awake.

So how do you know all this. Because it sounds to me like you made it up.

It's not important how I know. You don't need that information to get better. Some of us are here to help those retreating to their dreams, to show you how to live in this world now.

I know how to live. I'm getting by.

Are you? Listen to me—I can help restore what was taken from you by the Censor. Don't you want back what has been lost? To feel complete again? We can piece those fragments back together.

His head throbs. The Censor...I don't know. I can't think about that right now. I'm actually starting to feel kind of tired.

The professor stands. I should go. I've probably told you too much at one time. I apologize if I've made you anxious. But please consider what I have said.

Sure, I'll think about it. It's an interesting theory, at least. Goodnight, Professor.

Goodnight.

He shuts the door and goes to the bedroom to look for the dream book. It's possible the man has somehow entered his quarters and stolen it. But, no, he finds it in the drawer of his bedside table, where it always is. He opens it and reads the first entry.

"Went to work. Processed requests. Met E at the coffeehouse. Walked through tunnels back to quarters."

He scans the rest of the page and finds it filled with similar entries. Strange—he can't recall these dreams, though he knows he sometimes dreams about work. He pages further in and soon finds others he recognizes. After reading a few of them, he returns the book to the drawer.

He feels he's made an error by reading the dreams. As if he's somehow violated his other part, the part living such an active, varied life when he is not awake. He yearns for this other part. His desire to get closer to it nearly eclipses the mundane daily existence he finds himself inhabiting. And yet what the professor suggests sounds ridiculous.

7.

He misses the next few days of work due to lack of focus. He stays in his quarters, moving restlessly from the bed to the kitchen table and back. He drinks tea and tries to read but can only manage two or three pages before his mind shorts out. He thinks about what the professor said and wonders if it's true the damage could be repaired. And what if it were true. Would he ever really feel complete again? He didn't even know what that would mean, what it would feel like. So many years since the damage occurred—time spent adapting, compensating for loss, reconfiguring—all hard wiring now, impossible to rip out and replace. Besides, maybe normal is only an ideal better left behind.

He thinks about the river, moments not redacted yet which he still holds in quarantine within his mind. It's as if over time he became his own Censor, having internalized for so long the distorted moral compass of that rigid machine, programmed as it was to keep him on a path from which he could not stray for long before his wayward steps would be erased. But perhaps it's not too late to break free of this internal mechanism. The old damage from the Censor may remain, but if he could learn to stay open, not to close himself down at the moments of familiar panic, he might at least have a chance to approach normal, while still keeping in mind the impossibility of ever inhabiting it as a fully realized state. He has to at least make an attempt, for this stasis he lives in surely holds defeat. And defeat is a form of slow death he cannot bear.

To quiet his mind he lights the incense E brought him. He fits the end of the stick into the stone holder and watches as the smoke curls upward from the glowing ember at the tip. The fragrance of cedar soon fills the anteroom where he sits sipping his tea. This scent takes him away from the sterility of his quarters, back to a time before the Change. He stares into the wisps of smoke and sees shapes begin to form. Entire worlds are built and destroyed within the fine intricate movement of the smoke. Funnel clouds appear and drift apart into shreds. He thinks about the tree in the woods behind his old house. Would it smell like this if it were on fire? Maybe he should have burned it to the ground—a sacrifice made to anyone who cared to pay attention to what was happening around them. All the redaction and its end result: destruction on a scale far greater than the burning of a single tree behind a house the same as all the other houses nearby.

He breathes in the smoke and wishes he had the cinders left from the tree he now imagines he burned. They rest in a stainless-steel canister on his bedside table. Each night before he goes to sleep he unscrews the top and breathes in the scent of cedar ash. They are sacred, these remnants of a disappeared world. He dips his finger in the ash and marks a cross on each of his cheeks. He looks in the mirror and what he sees he no longer recognizes: someone with nothing left who is locked in a war with himself. One side thinks it remembers everything and the other side has forgotten all but a few pieces gleaming in the shadows.

He lies in bed now staring at the never-changing light. The artificial birds begin their programmed singing, right on time, as always. He listens, for their tuneless song is impossible to ignore. But now something is not quite right. One bird sounds off-key. He sits up, listens closer. Yes, there it is again. One bird is singing a completely different "melody" than the others. How bizarre. A glitch in the program perhaps, though such errors are virtually unheard of. This discovery unsettles him at a primal level. The bird continues on with its strange song, venturing further into even more discordant territory. His eyelids droop as he listens to the song, struggling to follow the pattern, until sleep overcomes him.

8.

He wakes up at his desk. Ever since he quit coffee he keeps nodding off at work. He takes a sip of water, sits erect in his chair. Now his fingers clatter across the keyboard. *Approve this, decline that, reply, delete, reply all, forward, wait for response, click check-boxes, click submit, arrows, buttons.* Work is entering the busy cycle again. Many credits to process. His fingers tap across the keys in a blur.

He does not go to the coffeehouse. It's too much temptation, being around so many others drinking coffee after he has quit. Instead he takes his break at his desk. He brings a book from the stack on his bedside table. He drinks herbal tea as he reads and he does not think about what happened on that day, about her thin brown hand and what it held. Neither does he think about E. He does not think about when he met her or where. Anyway, she is gone. She disappeared months ago or maybe last week. He cannot remember. He is not concerned.

At first he thought she might turn up again, knowing her shifty drifter ways. He kept returning to the coffee-house but she was never there. He knows now she will not return. He doesn't know how he knows it, but he is certain. And strangely it feels right, as if from somewhere else she's reassuring him he will be okay without her.

This morning he wrote in the new dream book. Last night he dreamed about an island in the middle of a lake. He was both living on the island and watching himself from a distance. An enormous cedar forest surrounded the lake. He saw himself row a small boat across to the mainland, where in the shallows tall reeds swayed erect in the morning breeze. He pulled the boat onto the shore and gathered dry wood from the forest floor. He tended a garden in a clearing bright with warm sunlight. He saw himself cross back over to the island and chop wood outside a tiny cabin. He cooked a simple lunch on a wood stove. As the sun set, he gazed at a thin plume of smoke rising from the cabin's chimney to an indigo sky fastened with Orion's Belt. He woke still smelling the sweet scent of cedar smoke.

At work he asked management to block his access to the faces inside squares. He told them it was for the best,

that without them he knew he could at least double his quarterly processing totals. It was not against policy to look at the faces inside squares. Everyone did it, even management. But for him it had always been about the search, and the urgency to find has fallen away.

He no longer believes his old professor lives in his building. But in the tunnels he sometimes thinks he sees the man or someone who looks like him, wearing a faded grey suit and a fedora—clothing so far out of fashion it's impossible to miss. The man smiles at him in a curious way. He nods back, in a rush, always, to return to his quarters, to take his vitamin D injection, to read his books, alone in the silent building, where others may live or not, he's still not certain. He still hopes to one day find out.

Dear ———— ,

I haven't left my "studio" in weeks. All I do is paint. The walls are covered with paintings. I've now run out of space and so I started stacking the canvases in piles. The paint isn't even dry and the canvases are sticking together. It doesn't matter. I'm awake all the time. Or asleep. I can't even tell anymore. I paint the tree, the river, the image from the textbook. Over and over I paint them in succession, varying the order, sometimes aligning them as a triptych, sometimes incorporating them all in a single canvas.

When F died I had to leave the city. I don't think you ever knew her, but she was dying from the condition. I'd been filming her dreams and giving her therapeutic aid. Remember how I never wanted to hear about your work? Maybe it was from guilt over never telling you about mine. But I wasn't licensed and I didn't want to mix you up in it. The professor led me on with the idea of an "apprenticeship" that he would guide me through as I continued working with my clients. Eventually I figured out he doesn't know much more than I do about the condition. He's mostly just talk.

I miss our conversations at the coffeehouse. As you told me that one day—the distance remains. It's unavoidable. But it doesn't matter if we're sitting across from each other or living in different cities hundreds of miles apart. Maybe I wasn't ready to admit that to myself when you said it. Now I know it's a central part of this experience. Heraclitus said each of us turns aside into our own darkness. It happens whether we're asleep and dreaming or awake and painting scenes from dreams and memories. That's the inexplicable nature of this condition—the source of it has grown too diffuse to identify. Yet we keep pushing forward even as everything real around us is replaced by the artificial. To give up altogether would mean defeat and defeat is a kind of death. But it's the kind of death that constricts a life without ever taking it. I don't want that kind of death. So all I can do is keep painting what I know is real. I hope you too have a way to keep what is real close to you.

Yours,

E

VOLUME II

PROLOGUE

I remember it was an overcast day. I was visiting you for the weekend. That is, my parents and I were visiting you and your parents. We'd gone shopping that day, at a collection of shops nested along interconnected concrete pathways lined with benches and planters. Yes, it was like that. It was designed the way downtowns used to be, before they were all abandoned.

We were together while our parents were off somewhere else. You saw a bookshop and wanted to go in. And so I followed. We didn't know each other well. It was one of those situations where two sets of parents are friends and so they expect their kids to be friends, too. Except I was a girl and you were a boy and we were both at the age where it starts to make a difference, except not everyone is aware of what kind of difference it makes. I think I was more aware of it than you.

So there we were, in the bookshop. The magazine rack was right inside the front door. I saw it first and I rushed over. You hung back, uncertain, perhaps cowed by my enthusiasm. I reached toward the top row and you looked over at the counter and back at me, softly pleading for me to leave it alone. C'mon, I said, don't you want to see. But you wouldn't even look at me. You stared at your shoes—turquoise Converse Chuck Taylors. I tried to convince you, grabbed your wrist and tried to pull you toward the back of the shop. But you'd gone rigid. It was like you weren't there anymore. And then the guy at the counter told us to leave so we did.

PART I

1.

I wasn't doing anything. I'd quit my processing job, or maybe I'd been "let go" as they say. Did it really matter which. I doubt it. Though it was true I'd become a liability after all the blackouts. So maybe they did find a way to get rid of me without violating any employment laws. But in the end I don't think it mattered. In my head I walked out of there of my own volition and never went back. I left everything in my office as it always had been, so it looked like I might come back at any time. Yes, it looked as if I'd simply stood up from my desk and left for the day and would be back the next morning, early like usual, before everyone else, so I could get my tea and my water and be comfortably situated when everyone else showed up. But in fact I did not return the next day or any day after that.

For years I processed requests from all over the globe. I granted people access to what they wanted—what they could not find anywhere else. I evaluated each request with care, ensuring the intended use fit within our stringent guidelines. If it did not I queried the requester and through our correspondence we often worked out an understanding. Sometimes we did not. Sometimes those making the requests were turned away empty-handed. But most of them got what they wanted. They were content, even ecstatic on occasion. And I made that happen. I was the gatekeeper.

Of course having this power wasn't enough to justify my continued presence there. I felt like I was disappearing. My work had no true meaning. I was too removed from the supposed difference being made in people's lives. Sure, they thanked me, sometimes profusely, but I was only a facilitator, a middleman. No one remembers the middleman. And beyond this essential deficit, it was also becoming increasingly difficult to accomplish my work at the professional level I insisted on maintaining. The fact is my superiors had no vested interest in my work. Their concerns lay in another realm. They did not want to invest the resources necessary for me to continue my work at a professional level. Of course they paid lip service to the importance of my work, but in fact it meant very little to them. And likewise did my continued presence in the halls of the office. In short, I was invisible to them. And so I left. Or was let go. Either way I am no longer there.

So I left the area and went somewhere else. I traveled through the enclosed cities for months. Eventually I returned to my own city. One day I found a way out and I arrived here. I didn't do much. Each morning I got up and meditated before doing my exercises. I ate breakfast. When I finished eating I washed the breakfast dishes. I boiled water and made a cup of herbal tea. I took the cup to the chair near the window where I sat for a while and stared out the window. Sometimes I tried to read. But my mind was usually too restless to read. So I sat and watched what was happening outside my cabin, which on most days amounted to very little. It was high summer and the birds were laying low. When I tired of sitting I left the island, paddling the tiny boat across the lake's placid surface to the mainland. There I would tend the vegetable garden for an hour before entering the cedar forest for my daily walking meditation. I returned to the island around noon and cooked my lunch. After eating I washed the lunch dishes. The remainder of the day I devoted to reading and reflection.

The blackouts had stopped. After I left work without returning the next day or any day after that I didn't experience another blackout. I was glad for this. The blackouts were frightening. But the connection between work and the blackouts remains unclear. As does the connection between them and what she showed me that day so many years before. The slip of paper in her small brown hand.

2.

Now I think of you in that shop, so certain in what I saw as your transgression. That day in green—later all in black, even your hair. Your parents, did they even know of your libertine exploits. You looked so innocent, not to mention your still young age. No one would have ever guessed. I certainly would not have.

As I sit here outside my cabin the cicadas begin their monotone chorus and I marvel at their annual return. That life of traveling through dingy tunnels by day and night seems so far off. To think I survived for so long living encapsulated in that sterile city is absurd. Of course I nearly did not survive. My survival was marginal at best. If I had stayed in my position I surely would have met my end. I'm not certain how. Perhaps the blackouts would have grown incrementally stronger and lasted longer each time until eventually I would have experienced the final blackout from which I would never return.

But what was it possessing you, I wonder. What was driving your actions that day. We entered the store, or rather I walked toward it and you followed. My intent was pure but at what point did the thought enter your mind. As soon as we entered you walked straight to the magazine rack. But was it a premeditated event in your mind. If so, you hadn't had much time to formulate it. I had not even known there was a bookshop in this place our parents had taken us. I had never even been to this place. I had no idea my parents knew of its existence, nor did I understand why they chose to bring us there that day. It was a strange place and I can't say I liked it. And your parents certainly could not have known of this place, for your family lived in another part of the country altogether.

So what caused you to reach up there and take it down. Or did you even take it down at all. Perhaps you just reached for it. Yes, you must have reached for it as I desperately tried to restrain you while keeping an eye on the man at the counter, whom at the time of our entrance was helping a customer. But, no, restrain is not the right word. Unless I mean verbally restrain. For I would not have touched you. I would not have placed hands on you.

Not then, not even in my mind. I barely knew you, though you had certainly assumed an air of immediate familiarity. Yes, you had assumed an air I found nerve-wracking and inappropriate, yet also intriguing.

You reached up there as I in a low voice begged for you to leave it alone. I was out of my mind with anxiety. By now the customer had left the store and we were alone with the man behind the counter. I could feel his eyes like flames licking at the back of my head. You tried to pull me further into the store, down a row of shelves, away from the man's steady gaze. But I couldn't move. I didn't want to. I felt so confused by your actions. Everything felt wrong and I was unprepared. I wanted to get out of there. I felt the heat growing in my face. And the man, seeing our struggle, cleared his throat and said we'd better leave. Rolling your eyes, you dropped my arm and flounced away, shoving open the door and walking out. The bell on the door tinkled as I watched you through the window. The man's head swiveled on me then. "You, too, kid. Time to move along." And so I went.

3.

I had begun taking everything as a sign, which is always problematic. And certainly the blackouts had been the most monstrous, the most unavoidable sign of all. The increasing resurgence in my mind of the scene with her—the one handing me the paper with her "artwork" scribbled on it—could not be ignored as a related phenomenon. My thoughts about it all scraped from my mind by the Censor. My memories: a jagged array of mismatched imagery, sound, and scent swirling into a cacophonous confusion destroying my equilibrium. I feel the urge to stand near the tree again, to slide my hand down its orange bark. Now I see the river's silvery light projected onto the underside of the bridge.

I remember. I fall. I crawl to the bed and lie there for days until I'm fired or I simply don't return. My office looks like I just stood up and left, like at the end of any other day. The machine sitting atop the artificial wood grain. The rows of books, the framed posters on the wall. Still intact, as if I'd merely gone home, planning to return again in the morning. And maybe that is what happened. Maybe it was not a conscious decision on my part after all. Not as if it matters. Now that I have receded into the background. Now that I have passed through to the interstices of life, the in-between spaces where no one ever looks. I think I'm fine with it.

It happened one day like this. I walked home through the wretched tunnels as usual. I clambered up through the hatch onto the gleaming floor of my building's lobby. My home, such as it was. A place where I only ever saw one other occupant—my old professor from university. A well-meaning man, or so it would seem upon first impression. He wanted to help me, said together we could restore what I'd lost. As if he knew what I'd lost and how far apart I was from it at that point. He didn't know. But this isn't about him. Not now.

I climbed out of the tunnels and I knew something was different. Always it was quiet in the lobby. But this day there was a low frequency humming. I heard it immediately, as my senses operate in a heightened state at all times. One could say they are constantly excited to the farthest reaches of their abilities. So much input at one time—at all times. It's distracting and often incapacitating (see also: blackouts). I could not identify the source of the sound. I entered the elevator and pushed my floor number. The door shut but the humming continued. The door opened at my floor and I exited onto the carpeted hallway. The humming maintained its consistent low tone. It was not unpleasant, but neither was it pleasant. It was atonal, machine-like—the kind of ubiquitous noise most people no longer notice.

When I reached the door to my quarters I observed a faint green light running parallel to the door frame. Actually it was not a single light. It was a series of blinking green lights, two rows of them, like the indicator lights on those readers used to deduct credits from a payment card. Except this was on a much larger scale. The door frame was close to seven feet high and the lights ran along one entire side of the frame—the left side, to be exact. My left as I faced it, that is. I reached out toward the lights but hesitated, thinking I felt a slight heat as they began to illuminate my hand. I drew back my hand and pulled my key out of my pocket instead.

But as I inserted the key I found it wouldn't turn in the lock.

At this point I looked around and of course there was no one in the hallway. There never is. For at least the thousandth time I looked around at all the other doors, each of which had a number on it. Why the numbers. What significance is the number if there is no one behind the door—no resident other than me in this building (and perhaps the professor). It felt exhausting to think about so I turned my attention back to my own door. I still heard the humming and in fact I imagined it had slightly increased in volume. I peered closer at the lights and now saw what appeared to be a thin gap in between the two rows, running the full length of the door frame. What is this gap, I wondered. I tried saying the question aloud, tentatively. Of course no one answered. But now the humming audibly increased and as I bent my head closer to the lights, I could hear it clearer. So, I thought, the humming is coming from inside the gap. I felt satisfied to have determined the source. As I continued straining to listen, I came even closer and my body shifted position so I was now standing perpendicular to the wall, the door, and the lights.

All at once several things occurred: the green lumi-nescence increased in brightness to a near-unbearable level, forcing me to look away; the humming grew so loud I could no longer think, forcing me to shut my mind down to the only extent possible; the gap widened, and I felt a force working on my body, pulling it toward the gap. Within seconds, not realizing exactly what was happening, I felt my entire essence being pulled through the gap and immediately emerging from its opposite end into what appeared to be an identical hallway. As I found myself standing in front of what still appeared to be my own door, I decided to try the key and this time it turned in the lock and the door opened. I entered the ante-room and felt a leaden feeling of tiredness wash over me. I shuffled across the floor into the bedroom and col-lapsed onto the bed where I fell asleep at once.

4.

I wake up in the cabin with an image in my mind of you reaching for the shelf on that day. We had sat together in the far rear seat of your parents' custom van. Your parents in front, my parents in the middle, and the two of us in the back. You wore green shorts and a green and white striped shirt. I don't remember what I wore. Just as I still don't know what you wanted from me.

The cabin is basic: a single room with a small kitchenette at one end and a wood stove in the corner. There is a wooden table where I eat my meals. A rocking chair stands near a window, close to the wood stove. That is where I read. A cot is positioned along one wall. That is where I sleep. Behind the cabin is an outhouse. That is where I evacuate. There is no running water but I built a small gravity-fed rainwater collection system to suit my needs. Lake water suffices for cleaning. A small solar panel provides minimal electric power, but I don't use it much. Living here feels as real as anything else.

I planted the garden so I would have food to eat. I planted it on the mainland because the island is covered in tall trees camouflaging the cabin, shutting out the sun. So I visit the mainland each day to gather firewood, tend the garden, and walk in the cedar forest. I walk in the cedar forest and I think about that day when we entered the bookshop. Or I try not to think about it. I try to bring my attention back to my breathing but it doesn't always work. Some days the scene replays in my head from the moment I wake at dawn to dusk when I fall onto my cot in exhaustion. Other days I walk in a state of complete emptiness and it is blissful. These days are few.

My arcane systems of organization and esoteric procedures keep me grounded. Or do they. I like to think so but perhaps they make me insane. I am no longer able to distinguish the difference between madness and whatever normal feels like, if it is indeed supposed to feel differently than madness does. Leading a hermetic existence limits one's judgment in such matters. But I doubt it matters. At a granular level I am surviving and that is something.

I am empty now. I have given everything away to the wind. I emptied myself the first time I felt the wind blow on my face after I left that other world behind. Into the wind I emptied myself. But when I think about it I have always been empty. What there has been to give has been illusory. I tried to give but in the end there was nothing. It is why I turned away from you when you reached up for the unknown. Inside I already knew. The map had been drawn and I was only following a plotted course. I do know this, despite not knowing what you sought from me, if anything other than to be either a witness to your exploits or a partner in their fulfillment. So my emptiness remains. It is why I am here now alone with nothing around me. I blend in. And yet I question if I am truly empty. For I still have these memories. The ghostly imprints of what I shrugged off yet linger.

5.

When I walk in the cedar wood I hear ravens croaking in the treetops. It is so strange to experience real birds again, instead of the artificial ones outside the opaque window in my quarters. I look up into the trees but see nothing, only hear the flapping wings of departure. How can something so large remain unseen. I know they follow me, the ravens. So perhaps I am not invisible, only camouflaged like them. They are curious but also shy and retiring. Maybe we have more in common than I would expect. We hold a mutual curiosity never to be fulfilled due to the shyness we also share. I am so used to this unfulfilled feeling I now consider it normal, and if I were to suddenly feel satisfied I doubt I would recognize or comprehend it.

The fact that I am alone does not concern me. It is an accepted fact. I created this solitude. I left that other world. It was not where I belonged. I only experienced that one feeling. Working in a dead archive for people with short memories drove me here. Processing requests for others I would never meet. Just names on a screen with their constant demands, giving nothing in return and even refusing to follow the simple terms of use they'd agreed to when they made their requests. It was madness and it had to end.

In the woods one day I found a door. Or I thought I found a door. It's not always easy for me to distinguish between what is happening now, what has already happened, and what I have imagined has happened. I probe each moment for clues to its origin. I believe I've been trying to approach the door for weeks. But every time I get close I can no longer see it. So now every time I enter the woods I excise all thoughts of the door from my mind. I walk in a random direction. I think about anything except doors. I hope by using this technique, or anti-technique, I will in time find myself in front of the door. I will find myself there and at the point of recognizing the door I will reach out and grasp the knob and turn. I may even walk through it.

Of course I wonder what would have happened if instead of turning away I had conspired with you that day.

How would this have altered the arc of development. Would we have bonded over our shared excitation— the sudden rushing thrill of doing something against everything the Censors represented. Because isn't that what this is about. I obeyed and you did not. I bowed my head in subservience, accepting my stunted fate. But not you. No, you went your own way. You answered to no authority. Somehow you eluded Censor control— I still don't know how. But I did not even envy you that. I was too far gone. I had not yet woken up to the electric truth pulsing around me. When I finally did it was too late. In fact it was so late I wonder whether it would have been better not to have woken up at all. To have stayed asleep might have been preferable to this restless semi-woken state.

And now these woods. What am I expecting to find in these woods. A door that may or may not exist. Is this all there is to find. It seems so banal. I have food and shelter. And all day I tread these inner pathways. It feels like too much. I have learned the songs of all the birds. They are wired so deep inside me now I don't even need to reach for their names when I hear them. Instead the names run alongside the pathways: a steady stream of avian companions accompanying me on my daily rounds. Titmouse, chickadee, nuthatch, wren. Vireo, tanager, wood-pewee. Raven, crow, jay. Haunting cries of the loons at dusk out on the lake. Falling asleep to the owls waking up outside my walls.

6.

Where are you now? Do you live in an enclosed city? Did I used to pass you in those filthy tunnels every day on my way to the dead archive? I never looked at people's faces so I would not have seen you. Everyone looked the same in the tunnels anyway. Why you have hooked yourself in my subconscious is a mystery. There have been so many others who have passed through and left no visible trace. Though perhaps they have left invisible traces. Yes, invisible traces compounded over time have formed the part of me now dying, out here in this nowhere place, among the cedars, hidden as I am on my island.

It feels like I have been here for a long time yet I've seen no signs of seasonal change. I walk in the forest every day and everything remains in its place. The sun rises and sets at the same times every day. My body is in tune with the rhythms of time working on me and yet I've had to make no minor adjustments. What is this place and why have I come here. Is it only to think of you and that day and what bearing it may or may not have had on who I am today. Or does it go beyond this. Each day starts so full of promise. I wake full of hope for the future but with each passing hour I descend further toward the utmost futility. The sinking sun brings the end-of-day dread, the way it used to before in the other place—the anticipation of another descent to the tunnels.

One can still feel lost in the place one always hoped to find. Beauty can come not to matter. Jagged fragments of memories pierce through a veneer of relative calm. When a cold breeze blows in off the lake, chilling me through to the marrow, as I sit on the steps to the cabin, I still cannot believe how much has been lost. I see your hand reaching up, your thin and delicate hand, poised to defy everyone with your plunge toward the unknown. I want to grasp it now and follow you there. But of course that is an impossible notion unworthy of consideration.

Your innocent looks belied your intentions. I was taken in. You took me into your world, or tried to. Fear of the Censor intervened and I resisted. I always resisted at that time. My resistance would cost me. One might say it has cost me everything. It is why I am now alone. Of course who is to say what "innocent" or "normal" looks like. Certainly I am not fit to make that judgment. But when I was younger I thought a different appearance could indicate a different way of looking at the world. Now that is all gone. Everyone looks the same and "different" has been commodified in myriad ways— repackaged and sold to whomever has the money to buy it. It doesn't matter.

I am here now and no one knows it. Wherever here is. This island. This cabin where I lay my head down at night. This mainland where I grow my food and walk in the cedar wood as the ravens tumble in the treetops overhead. This forest where there may or may not be a door, a door I may or may not have passed through to enter this place. I want to believe in it: the redemption granted me in the form of this paradise. But how do I know for sure. How do I reach the point where I am living without this constant oppressive awareness of everything around me. Awareness from which blooms only questions—an incurable virus of inquiry.

INTERLUDE

I remember it was a late summer day—heavy with a dim gray shade of overcast, the kind of day where if you pay close attention you might catch the first few hints of autumn. I was behind the counter helping a customer when they came in, the two of them. The boy walked in first, followed by the girl. She immediately brushed by the boy and rushed over to the magazine rack. I didn't think much of it at first. Kids are always coming in here and scoping the magazines. Usually I end up chasing them out because they rarely buy anything.

Anyway, so I was processing this customer's payment and not paying attention to what the kids were doing. There was no one else in the store. It had been a quiet day, especially for a weekend. I remember the customer was buying a large stack of hardcover bestsellers. I was quite pleased about this because it had been a particularly bad month for sales—one of those months where I really think hard about closing down the shop and trying a different gig.

As the customer was leaving I noticed the kids were kind of bickering over there in front of the magazines. I couldn't tell what they were up to. The girl grabbed the boy's arm and was trying to drag him out of my line of sight. I could see she had merchandise in her hand. But the boy wasn't moving. He was just standing there, rigid, staring at the ground. I have to admit it was a strange sight. But I wasn't interested in this drama going down in my store. So I told them to beat it. The girl flounced out the door and the boy followed, glancing back at me as he left.

PART II

1.

It happened. I found the door in the forest and I stepped across the threshold. You may wonder why. My life on the island was not a bad life. In many respects it was the best life I've ever led. I was 98 percent content. But the remaining two percent was destroying me. I started feeling a compulsion to find the door. This compulsion overshadowed my life, eating away at my imagined serenity. It haunted me day and night. As I watched the sunset an image of the door appeared in the sky, forcing me to contemplate its existence and wonder whether I should seek it out and walk through it. When I slept I dreamed of the door—of searching for it. Some nights I dreamed all night of searching for it and I never found it. I woke exhausted. Other nights I found it right away. But in my dreams I could never walk through it. I felt the resistance like weight bands strapped around my ankles, preventing my feet from moving forward.

One day I was out walking in the forest and the ravens were up above me as usual. At first when I arrived here they would flap their wings in alarm and disappear as soon as I approached. But since then they'd grown used to me and would stay in the canopy, croaking and chuckling. This time they were quiet but I knew they were there. I heard their soft rustling. After a few minutes a pair of them took flight but at a lower height so I could see them. As I had nothing else to do, I followed them. They flew deep into the forest to an area where I had never visited before. The trees were dense here but soon a clearing opened up before me. The ravens perched at the top of a snag at the clearing's edge and started making excited calls. I walked into the center of the clearing and the doorway suddenly materialized, hovering in front of me. The ravens were now flying frenzied around the clearing, their calls more agitated than I had ever heard them. I hesitated before the door but the ravens came closer, their wings beating in my ears, their feathers brushing against my arms, urging me forward. And so I grasped the knob and turned it.

After I crossed the threshold I found myself in the hallway outside my quarters. I looked around but as usual there was no one there. The building was silent like always. There was no humming noise. I opened the door to my quarters and went to the bedroom where I opened the drawer and took out the dream book. I wrote in it for a long time and then I sat on the bed staring at the never-changing light. I thought of you, of your arm extended, hand reaching up. The look on your face—what was it—excited determination perhaps. Your green eyes opened wide. Soon I grew tired. As I prepared for sleep I found a small steel urn on the bedside table. I lifted the lid and the scent of cedar filled the room, flooding my cerebral cortex with raw energy and causing me to black out. When I woke I heard the chirping of the artificial birds. A new day: time to return to work.

2.

At the office my superior does not appear surprised to see me. I feel uncertain. Every doorway takes me back to that day, entering the bookstore, your touch electric on my arm as you tried to pull me deeper into the stacks. I shake the sensations off each time and try to focus. Oddly I am in my old office now. Not what I think of as my current office with the unreliable machine clattering on the artificial wood grain. But the isolated office I used for a year in between previous project iterations. It was a time when funding was scarce. During that time I managed an archive, a collection of pamphlets, posters, various ephemera—all concerning the Change. The collection was established to house official documents from governments all over the world: safety guidelines, public health warnings, promotional materials from awareness campaigns. Text screamed off the pages: The Change Is Coming! Are You Prepared? Actually the literature was not so alarmist. Perhaps if it had been more people would have paid attention. Instead it contained innocuous-sounding terms like climate, population, and environment. The governments hadn't wanted to induce panic, though in retrospect they may have erred too far on the side of caution. It's so hard to say for sure.

During that year I spent hours online each morning scouring government portals and international news feeds for new material. I found intricate predictive models, case studies on early casualties, evacuation instructions, and checklists of emergency provisions to keep on hand, all of which I dutifully printed out, slid into acid-free protective sleeves, and filed in the appropriate drawers. The drawers are color-coded by region and organized alphabetically by country within each region. Using laughably outdated archive management software I created detailed catalog records for each material, including physical descriptions, annotations, and keywords for subject access. Sometimes I arranged displays for the suite's vestibule to highlight individual country response campaigns. It felt futile at the time but I needed to keep busy.

I step outside my office now and look around at the archive. Everything is still here. Even one of my displays sits sagging on a countertop. I wonder if anyone will ever use this material again. Will a time come in the future when researchers will seek out this information in an effort to understand what happened. After all, it is an impressive monument to governments doing what governments do best: producing and disseminating valuable information they must know will never be used by the majority of their citizens whom, when facing calamity, as they were with the Change, instead inevitably revert to their animal instincts in order to survive. Or at least they have in the distant and recent past. Perhaps one day far in the future new instincts will evolve and this entire period of our history will seem incomprehensible. But right now to imagine such a drastic shift is difficult.

3.

When I ask my superior about my office he makes a strange face and changes the subject. He wants to replace the machine in my office with a new one. The current machine is different from the one that sat atop the artificial wood grain. It's much older than that one, which was actually a recent model, albeit terribly flawed. This old machine I am using now is slow but at least it doesn't clatter or unexpectedly lose its network connection. It plods along executing its processes at a slow, steady pace. I don't mind the slowness, as it affords me plenty of time to daydream. But my superior is concerned about the potential drop in my productivity, despite not having told me what I'm to be working on. Presumably it is not the dead archive. There is nothing to be done with that now. It is frozen in time and as such only of interest to historians or perhaps to public health practitioners looking to prevent—or at least mitigate the effects of—

the next ecological disaster. Occasionally a request to see a certain material drifts in through the central help desk, but these are easily fulfilled by persons other than me, though for inexplicable reasons they often do still find their way to me.

I'm in no rush to find out what my superior wants me to do. If I had a choice I suppose I'd rather return to processing requests, as it would require the least effort on my part and change is always anathema to me, although I also cannot say for sure I want to spend long days processing again. I feel so vague, as if I'm only half here. I can't tell if people at the office are unsurprised to see me again or if they aren't completely seeing me. Maybe they are only seeing part of me, or sensing my presence but not clearly enough to acknowledge it, only enough to necessitate the shrugging off of an inexplicable queer feeling.

Mostly now when I daydream I think of you on that day in the bookshop. And what happened later in my room when we returned to my house. Your interrogation of me felt so alien. I never understood what you wanted from me. I still don't know. It generated a lifetime of unsated curiosity. And now there are the faces inside squares, pixelated representations of what may or may not occur juxtaposed with what may or may not have already, actually, occurred. There are also the faces in these hallways—unchanging—and the ones in the tunnels—the ones unseeable. So many faces there are and yet when I raise my hand to touch my own face I see my hand tremble, as if uncertain whether it will simply pass through air.

4.

Every morning has a certain feel to it, and this often dictates what actions are appropriate to take that day. The weather used to play a large role in setting a tone for the day. But now that we all live in a climate-controlled environment we have to look to other cues. I woke up this morning as usual to the chirping of the artificial birds. But something felt different. I can't explain it beyond a certain tingling in my extremities, the blood rushing faster in its vessels. Perhaps I felt more alive, more complete. I knew right away I would go to the coffeehouse. I had not been there since I returned. I didn't expect to find E but I thought if I sat there the way we used to sit there for so many hours maybe I would feel something—perhaps a premonition or an inclination to act in a way I had not previously considered.

I took a break from staring at the ancient machine struggling through its processes and went to the coffeehouse.

When you've been away from a place for so long there is always a heightened degree of anticipation as you approach it again. Will it look the same. Will I feel the same when I enter and re-experience what was once so familiar. I entered the coffeehouse in the throes of such anticipation. All appeared normal. I even thought I recognized some of the regulars from when I used to meet E there. I wasn't sure if this was a comfort or not. It made me wonder if other people's lives were on such vastly different trajectories from my own that I had no hope of ever relating to them.

I filled my cup with herbal tea and sat down at our old table. I had E's letter in my pocket. Of course I'd already read it multiple times. But I thought if I read it in the coffeehouse—the place where I spent the most time with E—that I might draw more insight from her words. I pulled out the single folded sheet of paper and read it again. It seemed I had not known much at all about how E had been leading her life. I felt sad about this but I also knew it had probably been for the best. Often the more we know about how someone else lives their life, the more inclined we are to judge and thus taint the purity of our connection with that person.

It interferes with the actual ongoing process of real-time learning about another person. It did not bother me how E had kept this significant part of her life from me but knowing it now made me feel helpless. If I had known maybe I could have helped her and then I would not be sitting alone in the coffeehouse.

The part of E's letter about the professor leading her on with promises of an apprenticeship did not surprise me. I had determined on my own the man's erratic nature. It's actually kind of funny to think how we talked about and almost around him, although I remember now how E had downplayed the man's significance, in what seemed to have been a deliberate manner. I wonder if she had been tempted to tell me more about the man's unreliability. What would have happened if she had told everything to me. I could not imagine the consequences.

E had not included a return address on her envelope. She may have been feeling paranoid. I'm not sure why she would have wanted to keep her location hidden from me, but she could have at least included it in the letter itself. I read over the letter again. She talks about "the condition" as if it's something identifiable within the population. Of course there has been no word from the government about this so-called "condition." It could even be related to the Censors.

After work I enter the dingy tunnels and traverse their bleak circuitry. They are the same: the orange electric lighting illuminates the dank walls dripping with condensation. The throngs pass by—heads down—faceless masses resigned to this daily horror. Before, my anxiety levels would be surging, but now I feel only numbness. I climb up the ladder to my building and cross the lobby to the mailroom, my heels clicking on the marble floor. There is no one in the mailroom. Where is the professor. Long gone, maybe even from the city itself, or struck down by the condition. Where is everyone else—an old question. I feel too tired to even wonder anymore.

Out in the lobby again I pause to observe the warm yellow light emanating from the art deco sconces mounted on the walls. It strangely pleases me, here, in this isolated location—a barren building lobby in the middle of this enclosed city. I feel a sensation akin to home, but as if I am feeling it from a distance, as through a dense fog, or more observing rather than feeling it. I shrug it off and take the elevator up to my floor.

Inside my quarters I prepare kitchari and eat slowly, allowing the flavors of each bite to fully awaken in my mouth. Afterwards I sit at the table drinking tea. I take out E's letter and reread it. She mentions this woman F whom she had been helping. I do not think I know her nor do I think E ever mentioned her before. The woman died from the condition. Who was she? I feel a strange kinship with this dead woman. Part of it is related to the idea of the condition as something I might share in common with others. But it also feels even deeper.

5.

My superior has assigned me a new project. I am to catalog several thousand pre-Change digital photographs of the natural world. It's a small contract awarded to my organization by the Federal Department of the Environment, now a tiny agency primarily occupied with historical research. Naturally I am thrilled; given the circumstances, looking at photos of nature is a suitable replacement for experiencing it firsthand. While I wait for the files to transfer onto my ancient machine, I sit at my desk daydreaming about all the possibilities waiting for me in these images. Perhaps there are even images of a cedar forest...and ravens.

When I begin reviewing the images I am surprised at their diversity. Not only are there photos of long-extinct birds and other animals, but also of people who lived in previously thriving natural areas all over the world. One portrait of a young girl who lived on a remote island off the coast of a tiny rural country captivates me. I zoom to the maximum resolution and stare into her eyes, mesmerized by the yellow-green, almost reptilian cast to her irises. I know I've seen a similar look. Feral yet expectant—a layer of domestication hidden beneath the wildness. When my superior stops by to confirm transfer of the images, I hurriedly close out the file, suddenly self-conscious of indulging in my rapture.

I take a break and go to the coffeehouse. Of course it's not the same without E, but regaining these elements of the familiar helps to ground me. Ground me in what I'm not sure. Do I really want to grow accustomed to this life again—the inexorable daily routines that nearly drove me mad. But there were also the flashbacks, the blackouts, and the endless dissection of that scene, of her handing me the paper with her drawings on it.

I dispense myself a cup of coffee substitute and sit at the usual table—the one I used to sit at with E. I stare at the door leading to the tunnels, half hoping she will show up and walk toward me, all heads swiveling to watch her, a tall reed refusing to sway. But she is not coming, not today. I drink my coffee substitute, imagining the ghost of a caffeine rush in my veins, and wonder where she is, what she is doing.

Today I feel the start of the slow crawl toward the torpor of the winter months. Despite the lack of seasonal change manifesting itself in a physical manner, I still feel it at times. Particularly so in what is now "winter" in name only. That sluggishness filling my veins, a languorous reaching for long novels to fill interminable gray hours. Even though the days are not actually shorter— the absence of natural light preventing that phenomenon —and instead all the hours are gray, every last one all year round, I still feel it.

I finish my drink and return to work, where I find my superior standing outside my office.

I have someone I'd like you to meet, he says. Our funder amended the contract to include a half-time employee to assist with cataloging the images. I'd like you to train her and afterwards you will oversee her progress.

Fine, I reply. Even though inside I am disturbed at the prospect of an outsider encroaching on what I'd understood to be my own solo work.

He leads me to a cubicle down the hall. The new employee's name is N. She has a recent degree in archives management. Of course our first encounter is awkward. I am terrible at meeting people. I don't know how to conduct small talk and I speak softly so I am often forced to repeat myself. N also looks oddly familiar to me, which I find distracting, if not highly troubling. Luckily she also appears quiet so I am hopeful we'll be maintaining a placid, distanced working relationship. Perhaps she will only now and again at the very beginning approach me for a point or two of clarification, which I will then respond to in a swift, efficient manner, after which we will both return to our respective desks to work quietly for the duration of this contract. I may even be able to convince myself I am working on my own, even when in fact I am not.

I return to my office and sit down at the ancient machine. It hums on the artificial wood grain. To accompany my existing monitor, my superior has dredged up an enormous wide screen monitor so I may enlarge the images to ridiculous proportions. This monitor makes me nervous—I feel it is sending out massive pulses of radiation immediately absorbed into my body where they wreak havoc in my cellular structure, distorting it into precancerous designs to lie dormant for years until one day suddenly multiplying into legions.

I click through a few images and type up some cursory notes before becoming distracted by my wandering thoughts. Will E ever return. And what about F. Why do I feel this connection to someone—now supposedly dead—whom I never even met. A feeling like I should be doing something on a grander scale than cataloging photos comes over me, destroying my concentration, sending me on disparate reveries from which I feel I'll never return.

6.

A few days later N comes to my office. I have not seen her since our first awkward meeting. I have no idea what she has been doing, but I assume it probably involved paperwork, orientation, human resources nonsense. I point her toward the only other chair in the office.

I have a message for you.

What do you mean...from our superior?

No. It's from E.

She looks nervous, as if she's not sure I'm the right person to receive the message.

From E.

Yes.

I'm tempted to close the door but don't wish to arouse suspicion, in her or anyone else. So instead I lower my voice almost to a whisper.

And so how do you know E.

I come from another city. I met her in a coffeehouse where I used to go between classes while I was working on my degree. E was often there at the same time. One day she asked if she could sit with me, and we started talking. This went on for a few months until I was hired for this position. When I told her about it she said she knew someone who used to work here. She wasn't sure if you still did, but she asked me to give you a message if you were here.

I see. Well, that is some story. Quite a coincidence.

N shifts in her seat. Do you not believe me.

I'm not sure. I suppose I have no good reason not to believe you.

Well, E specifically said I should not tell you here. That we should go to the coffeehouse nearby where you two used to meet.

And so we go to the coffeehouse. As we walk through the tunnels I feel a mixture of skepticism and elation. I don't even notice the slimy walls, the faceless masses tromping past us. Suddenly we are there in the brightly lit coffeehouse. I am dispensing a cup of tea. I glance at N and the expression on her face is serene. She is radiating energy. We sit down at a table and she begins to speak in an arcane dialect I remember my old professor using in class one day.

I interrupt her. Look, I don't understand what you are saying. I mean, I recognize some of the sounds you are making, I've heard them before, but I don't know what the sounds mean.

Her face falls. Oh. I just thought, I mean, I expected you knew. The message E gave me, she told it to me this way.

Well, I don't know why she would have done that. She knows I don't understand this way of speaking. So, can you translate it?

I'm not sure. It's not that easy. There are concepts within the message with no corresponding equivalent in our language. The one-to-one connection is just not there and I'm not sure I'm skilled enough to compensate.

I see. I suppose I have no other choice then but to try to locate the professor.

The professor?

Just some man who I used to think lived in my building. A former teacher of mine at university. He knows this dialect and perhaps could translate the message. Are you willing to come to my building this evening after work, say around 7?

I guess I could do that.

Please, will you do it or not? This is important, N.

She smiles. Okay, yes, I will be there.

I write my building address on a napkin and hand it to her.

I'll be waiting in the lobby.

I return to the office and stare at the twin screens, unseeing. Again I feel troubled by the seeming familiarity of N. At one point I feel a blackout coming on. For a moment I see you—a flash of your arm moving, reaching upwards. My eyes glaze over, I see static. I grip the edge of the desk until the feeling passes. Afterwards I feel cold sweat breaking out on my forehead. I am suddenly exhausted. I tell my superior I'm feeling unwell and return to my quarters, passing almost alone through the tunnels.

7.

When I exit the elevator into the lobby at precisely 7, N is already there. She is staring at one of the art deco sconces on the wall. I approach her.

This is an old light fixture, she says.

Yes, the entire building is a replica of one from the 1920s. Or so I've been told.

A replica? How strange. Why is it not authentic?

I'm not sure. Perhaps it is. It's only what I've been told. Or rather what I read in the sales brochure prior to moving into my quarters.

Have you lived here long?

Many years. I've lost track of the exact number, though it no longer seems important. Shall we go look for the professor?

In the elevator I press the button for the 15th floor, recalling the last time I had done so. It seems so long ago, though maybe in increments of time it has not been so long. I went away and came back. E went away and has not returned. At another time the professor tried to help me and I eschewed his aid. Now here I am attempting to seek it in earnest.

Following an awkward silence the elevator stops again at the 14th floor. We get out and I lead N to the emergency stairwell. We stand in front of the door that does not look like a door, but more like a wall. N places her hand on it, as I had done when I first came here on my own. She slides her hand down the surface of the door, or wall, to the point where a doorknob would typically be. When she removes her hand a doorknob appears. She reaches out and turns it. I notice she is smiling. We pass through and find another set of stairs leading up. At the top of the stairs is another door, this one with a knob. Again I defer to N who turns the knob and passes through the doorway. I follow and we find ourselves inside a bright white loft. Aside from some sparse furnishings, it is devoid of anything resembling décor.

At the far end of the long room the professor stands staring out a window at the never-changing light. As I look around the room, I can't help thinking this floor plan wasn't included in the building's sales brochure. Finally N clears her throat and the professor turns to us.

What can I do for you.

I need your help.

I see. Unlike when last we met and you decided you didn't want it.

It's not that I didn't want it. I just thought I'd be fine on my own.

And were you?

Yes and no. It's not important now. Look, this is N, gesturing toward her. E sent me a message through her, but I can't understand it.

Ah. And are you sure you want me to learn the contents of this message? E and I did not exactly part on good terms.

Well, I don't have much of a choice. You're the only one I know who can translate it.

He nods and sweeps his hand out in front of him, beckoning N to start her recitation. As she begins her singsong chanting I go to the window and stare out at the never-changing light. From far below I hear the faint chirping of the artificial birds. I think of the cabin for the first time since I returned. I say "returned" not even knowing what this means. Did I even leave and, if so, what have I left behind and to what have I returned.

After N finishes I turn to look at the professor. He is staring at a fixed point of uncertain location across the room. There is nothing across the room except a blank wall. Across from it, behind the professor, sits a beige settee, centered against the wall. Along the windowed wall behind where I am standing there is an armchair, a small wooden table, and a floor lamp. N stands in the middle of the room, as if she were on a stage. The soft glow of a recessed light in the ceiling falls across her face.

I clear my throat and the professor looks at me. He first nods then shakes his head. His constant affectations rankle me. I cannot believe I have debased myself by coming here and asking for his help.

Perhaps we should sit. He gestures toward the armchair.

I sit down and he sits on the settee. N looks around her before walking over to join the professor on the settee. There is nowhere else for her to sit.

At this the professor jumps up, as if suddenly remembering his sense of decorum.

Could I get either of you something to drink? I have red wine or bottled water.

He looks down at N, who shakes her head.

Please, I say. Can we get to the point? I would like to know the meaning of the message.

He sits down again, his hands fluttering in his lap.

Right, so...it seems E has, er, rather she *thinks* she has discovered something regarding the condition. A way to slow or even stop progression of it.

He breaks off.

Well, I say. That's not all, is it?

I don't agree with her.

That's not important to me. I want to know the entire message.

The professor's eyes flash.

I don't think you do. And I don't have to tell you.

I look at N, who rolls her eyes.

For a moment I consider threatening him, but I have concerns over his possible associates.

Fine. You're right—you don't have to tell me. But let me remind you of how desperate you were to help me before. I didn't think I needed your help then, but I'm asking you for it now. Please.

It pains me to have to prostrate myself before this loathsome man but I feel I have no other recourse. I turn away from him toward the window, straining to hear the artificial birds. It sounds as if one is singing a different melody, just like before, what seems like so long ago. For a moment I forget about the professor and focus instead on this aberration.

Do you hear that?

Hear what, N asks.

The birds. One of them is singing a different song.

I don't hear anything.

I look at the professor. He is staring across the room again. I feel the heat rising inside me. I force myself up out of the chair. I've had enough of his nonsense.

Well, then, I guess we'll be leaving. I hope you'll change your mind. If so, you know where my quarters are.

The professor doesn't answer. It looks as if he's in a trance. I walk up to him and snap my fingers in front of his face. He shakes his head a few times then clears his throat.

I'm sorry I can't help you, he mutters.

We exit to the stairway. In the elevator I ask N if there is anything she can tell me about the message, any kind of rough translation.

He is telling the truth about E. She thinks there is a way for people to free themselves of this condition.

Why didn't you just tell me that before.

Because I don't understand any of it. I had no idea what E was talking about when she gave me the message. All I knew to do was to relay it in the dialect in which it was told to me.

But now you are able to confirm what the professor says.

Well, yes. It's different now. Hearing it summarized in the way he did allowed me to do so. I couldn't do that in my head at first. But I have some context now.

Fine, that's fine. I don't understand but I have no reason not to believe you.

Please, she says, touching my arm.

I recoil at her touch and she turns away, staring up at the descending floor numbers.

I guess I will just see you at the office.

Yes, I'll see you tomorrow.

I exit the elevator at my floor and walk to my quarters. I think of you in the store that day. Your green and white striped shirt. Your self-assured smile. The easy laugh spilling from your lips. As I slip the key into the lock I feel dizzy. I place my other hand against the door to steady myself. Once inside I make tea and sit at the table, listening to the artificial birds. They sing once again in harmony.

8.

I wake from a dream thinking about F, this woman I don't think I even know, except from what E has written to me. In the dream I am in the strip of woods behind the houses on my old street. I'm standing near the tree with orange bark. I hear the crunching of dry leaves underfoot and I crouch down low behind some bushes. I can see through the branches to the tree. A girl approaches and reaches out to the tree, sliding her hand along the smooth bark and into the moss-covered cleft between the split trunks. Just beyond the woods there is a yard and a boy stands there, closer to the house than to the woods. The girl leaves the tree and walks out of the woods, crossing the lawn toward the boy. I see them speaking and she hands something to him. He looks at it for a moment then turns quickly to look up at a window of the house. There is a slight movement visible from within. Agitated, the boy says something to the girl, pointing toward the path running parallel to the side of the house. She walks away, turning back once to him, but he has already hurried inside.

At work I sit in my office and stare out the door at the dead archive. I think about the dream and wonder if E will ever return. I am irritated about how the evening at the professor's quarters transpired. I need E's insights into the condition. I need her to tell me what is happening to me. N has confirmed she has new information to share. So why is she not here yet. Why is she making me suffer like this. Unless she has sent N as her intermediary. Perhaps there is more locked within N than she is letting on, or even knows herself.

On a break from doing nothing other than obsessing over these things, I invite N to join me at the coffeehouse. N also does not take caffeine and so we sit silent, both drinking our herbal tea. I cannot figure out how to unlock this person. Admittedly I have never been good at forging initial connections with others. N does not look particularly expectant. She placidly sips her tea and looks around at the other patrons in a discreet manner. Her manners are impeccable.

I feel myself untethering again. I wonder if N can tell. I look at her and see no alarm present in her expression.

What are you feeling, I ask.

Nothing. And you?

Panic and dread.

She cocks her head. And is this normal?

It comes and goes. But right now I must leave.

She nods and I escape into the tunnels. Down there I notice the paintings right away. Three of them, one right after another, hanging on the dank walls. No one else seems to see them or maybe they don't even care to look. Same downcast eyes, feet shuffling, rustling of outerwear. It's difficult for me to see detail in this tight space, no room to stop and try to focus, the constant forward motion, panic rising. I duck into an alcove, stare across the passageway: it's her work, I know it is. The tree, the river, and what else...what is it...so familiar...the darkened centers...can it really be that. I feel myself falling, the old sensation, sliding down the slimy concrete wall.

I wake up, crumpled in the alcove—feels like only seconds later, but I look at my watch and see it's been longer, several minutes at least. I stand with difficulty, stumble to the ladder leading to my building. In the lobby I pause to catch my breath. As I stand there, leaning on the concierge's counter, the elevator door opens and the professor walks out. I make no move to greet him but he sees me and comes over.

Well, you look worse for wear.

Thanks. I'm trying to cultivate that look so I'm glad to know it's working.

What happened to you?

It's nothing. You know I have these spells.

Ah yes. The condition...

I don't want to discuss it with him so I make a move to leave, but he extends his arm, barring my way.

Say, you haven't heard from E, have you?

Only the message through N, why...

Oh, no reason. Just a hunch she might be returning to our fair city.

Why would she come back. There's nothing here for her.

Well...you're here, he says, his smile raising my bile.

She wouldn't return just for me.

Oh, he says, fingers fluttering, I wouldn't be too certain of that.

What do you know of it, I say, my teeth gritted.

But he just smiles again, his eyes rolling toward the ceiling.

Irritated, I turn away from him and hobble toward the mailroom.

Always nice to see you, he calls.

9.

I can't stand it anymore. Why did I come back here. Why did I have to go looking for that door and walk through it. No blackouts in that other place. But the two percent remained. Existence of the door. Awareness of somewhere else—a place I used to inhabit, a place where I went to the coffeehouse every day and sat with E— a tall reed refusing to sway—a set of lines, center-tangled. I could never staunch the flow of that awareness. Though it slowed to a trickle, it never dried up. And now...now I see this carefully wound gyre is bound to unwind. It may happen slowly but it has already begun and now it will never stop until it is completely unraveled.

Everything seems so far away, as if I am below the surface and seeing it all through murky green water. Nothing reaches me fast enough. There is always a delay—a refraction to allow my perception. Disconnected to the point of feeling as if a part is missing—or not feeling at all. There is a name for something like this in the annals of psychiatry. Neurologist Jules Cotard first observed it, describing it as Le délire des négations ("The Delirium of Negation"). So they named it after him. Cotard's syndrome. What a state to have named after you.

Today when I scan my key card and enter the suite, N is loitering in the dead archive, peering at some of my bygone displays warning of the effects of the Change.

Good morning, I say as I walk past her toward my office.

Wait, will you tell me about all this stuff?

I walk over and pick up a pamphlet about rising sea levels.

There's not much to tell. All of this material was produced by various governments and nonprofit watch-dog agencies to warn people of ecological collapse.

Weird. I don't remember seeing any of it when I was growing up.

I laugh. It was too late then. Didn't you grow up in an enclosed city?

She looks away. I'm not sure. There's a lot I don't remember from when I was a kid.

Oh. Well, I don't think these campaigns had their intended effect. There were also distribution problems. To be honest, I don't remember any of it from my childhood, either.

So, you organized all this stuff yourself?

I look around at the dusty displays, the neat rows of pamphlets, the framed posters on the wall.

Yeah, I did. It seems like a futile exercise now. Like so much of my life has been. It's hard to be here again, surrounded by it all, knowing no one will ever use it. It's like working next to a colossal monument to my own purposelessness.

I don't know what to say. I wish things were different for you.

You don't have to say anything.

Did E help you at all?

What do you mean?

With your purposelessness.

I laugh again, thinking about the years of circular conversations I had with E.

I'm not sure. I think she tried to help me, but I might have already been beyond help when I first met her. Why do you ask?

I don't know. I'm trying to get to know you, I guess. But it's not easy. You're so closed off.

Yes, that's what E always said. Part of it is the condition, you know...

Do you really believe such a thing exists? It seems like an excuse to me.

What do you mean?

So, people say they feel this gulf between themselves and other people. That they can't connect, but do they even try?

I think it's more complicated. Besides, the inability to connect is just one part of it, a symptom of a larger problem.

Well, it seems to me that people have retreated so far into the artificial they have drawn invisible lines around themselves. But maybe it's only a matter of willpower whether they cross those lines or not. They may have created a self-fulfilling prophecy. They believe they can no longer relate to other people and so they don't. If they took just one small step, though, they might surprise themselves.

I think about what she is saying. At first I scoff in my mind at what I perceive to be her naiveté. But this is the negative thinking at work. The immediate jump to judgment, to condemnation of an opinion other than my own. It is not constructive. Who are you, N, and why are you here.

She continues to stand expectant, waiting for my response. I am not sure I have one beyond the most obvious I hesitate to reveal. Yet I begin to speak, averting my eyes from her quizzical gaze.

There is something else about me, something that happened while I was growing up. The Censor's programming...it, well, it disrupted the way I developed.

I watch her open her mouth to reply as those years of repression flood my memory. I begin to feel dizzy and reach out to support myself on the counter.

N looks alarmed. Are you okay?

It's nothing. I have these spells sometimes. I'll just get to my office and I'll be fine.

She walks with me down the hall, makes sure I get to my desk. When she leaves I slump in my chair, scenes of that day with you in my mind—the bookstore, the ride home, my bedroom. I feel helpless, prickling heat rising to a head stuffed with cotton wool. I flick the power switch on the huge monitor and begin reviewing the day's batch of images.

10.

I'm in the alcove again, staring across at the paintings.
I know they are hers. Who else could have painted
them. It's what she wrote in the letter: painting the tree,
the river, the image from the old textbook she found
in another city. All of these are here now, in sudden
exposure on the tunnel wall, like ancient artwork discovered in some forgotten cavern. And the times they tell
of are far in the past, though not civilization's ancient
history, but maybe my own ancient history, yes, certainly
they are from that history. A time of uncertain heat, of
furtive movements in the woods, of snow melting on the
riverbank, the shadows racing underneath the bridge.

Could she really be back in this city? How else
could these paintings have gotten here? I would
have noticed them before if they'd been here longer.
Even though I keep my eyes down like all the others,
I could not have missed this. Yet no one else seems to

pay them any attention. Is it like N says—that they have merely willed themselves not to notice their surroundings? They have decided there is no longer anything worth observing, so they do not even see when something unusual appears.

E, where are you. I thought I would never see you again and it strangely felt right. But I am clearly not well, and neither is anyone else. Except for N. She remains unaffected. Is she right and everyone else wrong? Is she another anomaly, like the bird outside my window? She looks so young I'd assumed she'd been born after the Change, free of Censor intervention. Yet she claims to not remember much from growing up, which could imply Censor control. Also she knows the dialect, which would be highly unusual for someone born after the Change. She seems ageless to me. She lives in real time. I never see her plugged in. She eschews the artificial. Where could she have come from...

I leave the alcove and walk through the tunnels to my building. Everything is the same. There is no escape from it. My heels strike the marble floor of the lobby, ringing out loudly in this hollow space. I enter the mailroom and find the professor checking his box. I feel like

I am on a repeating loop. He turns to me.

Oh, it's you. So have you seen the paintings?

Yes, I've seen them.

And?

And what?

Do you recognize the motifs? From your episodes at the edge.

And what would you know about that?

You're always resisting our help.

Our help?

Yes, mine and E's. You're never willing to accept that we are only trying to help you.

I don't believe you. Maybe E has tried to help me. But you have only acted like you wanted to.

I don't know what you're talking about.

The message from E. You wouldn't even translate it for me.

Oh, that. Well, that was something altogether different. It didn't particularly concern you.

What? That's absurd. It very clearly concerns me.

Look, you are only one person among many suffering from the condition. It's not your role to understand this at the macro level. I have offered my services to you.

I said I would help you retrieve what was lost from the Censor. To heal your broken mind. It was a personal favor I offered you. But you refused it.

Maybe I didn't trust you then. At the time I was in worse shape than I am now. Besides, why would I want you to help me with that when E could do it just as well? She trained under you...she should know how to help me and I would be a lot more comfortable with her recording my dreams than with you doing it.

Hmm. That's not what I understand from her.

What do you know of it? She told me you didn't even follow through. So again, why should I trust you?

E was only a trainee. We didn't see eye to eye. She showed promise, but she is too idealistic. She thinks the answer lies in the herbal remedies, in behavior modification. That anyone can recover, even the worst cases.

And you? What do you believe? That I'm a lost cause, like that woman F?

The professor frowns. What do you know of her?

I know nothing. Only that she didn't survive.

Yes, she was an advanced case. Tragic, really. If we'd gotten to her earlier, perhaps...

It sounds like you set E up to fail with that case.

He glares at me. I would never do that. Anyway, I did not refer F. I'm not sure where E came across her, but I knew nothing of her before E began asking me for advice about her case.

I don't think I believe you.

Well, that is your prerogative. Now, I must take leave of you. I'm expecting a guest at my quarters.

He walks out and stands waiting for the elevator. As I watch him through the mailroom window I see his lips moving as if he's reciting an incantation. There's something not right about the man, but he's so evasive I can never be sure what it is or if I am only imagining it. I wait for him to get onto the elevator before walking out and pushing the button myself.

In my quarters I light the last stick of cedarwood incense and think about the ravens. I consider how likely I am to ever see or hear a raven again. I have no choice but to conclude the chances are slim. I think about your transgression. I see a small brown hand reaching toward me, a slip of paper between its slender fingers. The aching loss begins in my chest and rises through my throat, escaping in a low moan, drowned out only by the artificial birds outside my window, now chirping at night instead of morning.

INTERLUDE

I hated that place they took us. The shopping plaza made to look like downtown. The benches neatly placed in between huge concrete planters stuffed with colorful annuals. It was so artificial—the way everything else was heading, even then. I don't know why my parents chose to take your parents there, and to drag us along with them. I remember being so nervous, not knowing you well, but with this sense of expectation pervading the day.

I've always liked bookshops, though I prefer used ones. I often visited them with my dad, who could easily spend hours in any bookshop. I was always right there with him, but my mom never had the staying power. At the time used bookshops were in decline, but at least this shop, though only selling new books, was independent and looked to have a decent selection.

So we went in and right away I noticed the owner glowering at us from the counter. The guy made it plain he hated kids, especially when unaccompanied by an adult. You walked straight to the magazine rack and when I saw what you were reaching for I told you not to. It was an automatic response. You looked shocked at first, but you quickly began trying to convince me to go in the back, away from the prying eyes of the guy at the counter. I didn't even consider it. I shut up and looked down at the floor. You grabbed my arm and tried pulling me, but then the owner told us in a loud voice we either needed to buy something or leave. You sighed and rolled your eyes before walking out. I followed, drowning in a warm sea of relieved humiliation.

PART III

1.

I wake up in my cabin on the island. Even in the predawn gloom I recognize my surroundings immediately, so familiar they had become to me while I was here before. The first singing songbirds, seasonal visitors from the tropics, signal the time of year. But summer's evening chill common in this northern region still hovers. I shiver and wrap myself in the covers, picking out each of the feathered vocalists in my mind as they take their solos on the other side of the wall. Now a wood thrush steps up to the microphone, its ethereal fluted tones filling the new dawn air. How I have come to be here again feels unimportant —only a distant nagging mystery waiting patiently to be investigated and perhaps one day even solved.

Morning's inevitable pull toward action finally draws me up from my pallet. A weak grey light suffuses the room as I stand and stretch my body on the bare wood floor. As I move through the familiar poses, my

last memory before I woke reaches my conscious mind: hearing the sound of those demented artificial birds. I laugh, and as if in response an ovenbird utters its ringing "teacher, teacher, teacher" song somewhere from the forest floor. The real birds outperform the artificial ones every time, even when the latter begin to ad lib in a marked deviation from their programmed course.

The fragrant air, resinous with the scent of pine, fills the cabin. I prepare my modest breakfast, feeling lightness in my body, as if my bones are as hollow as those of the birds singing in the trees above. My movements are fluid as I slice through fresh berries harvested, somehow I know despite having no memory of it, from my patch on the mainland the day before. I feel no rush, no oppressive weight on me as I so often do when alone in my quarters in that so oddly silent building where I still think I live...I'm just not sure.

Am I only playing a role in this other reality? It feels so real, and my place in it feels natural. I move through it without thinking, but knowing what to do. Yet I am still cognizant of my existence in the enclosed city where I have toiled for so long, alongside my dead archive. I eat my breakfast now, savoring each bite, feeling a sudden awareness pierce the veil between these two places I inhabit, if indeed I do inhabit both of them.

I open the door and gaze upon the lake as the sun now crests the horizon, spilling the first rays of golden light across the lake's silvery surface. Such beauty arrests movement, demands attention. From me, at least, though not so much the wood turtle plodding across the front "yard," wholly invested in its slow, dogged determination to reach an unknown destination. With the sun's arrival comes a mixed crowd of chickadees and titmice to forage in the cabin's gutters. Their cheerful chatter as they feed inspires me to prepare for my own foraging expedition to the mainland.

I gather my baskets and shove off in the boat, rowing with ease across the narrow channel between the island and the mainland. A heron feeds in the tall reeds close to shore. As I approach, it lazily opens its wings and flaps off, legs dangling, toward a less popular locale. I pull the boat ashore and set off for the garden.

2.

With my morning's harvest stored in the cabin I take a break and sit on the small porch. The sun is higher in the sky and the birds have quieted down. When I consider the myriad ways of filling a day, I often turn first to the songbirds in my research. They follow a pattern. This becomes apparent if one stays in one place to observe them for an entire day. The songbirds first wake with exuberance to participate in the dawn chorus. Thereafter, their post-breeding days seem to consist of intervals of feeding and resting, with the middle of a summer's day being the least active time for them. As I observe this, I feel this middle of the day period myself as a heavy morass, its taffy-like consistency stretching out long-fingered minutes into thick, impermeable hours. Best to rest now, the birds whisper to me. Better to slip away into a dream, and return later to savor the late golden hours before the sun bows out after another day, ceding the stage again to the moon and stars.

Inside the cabin I cook a hearty lunch and devour it with gusto, feeling my digestive fire stronger than it's been in months. It feels good to eat this fresh food, grown just across the channel, thriving with the sun's energy. Afterwards, I spend a couple of hours chopping wood, for winter will not be long in arriving, though I cannot say whether I will be here. But I must prepare all the same, for without a supply of wood there will be no existence here for me.

As the late golden hours diminish, the crepuscular creatures filter into the gloaming, edging along the shadows, unwilling to fully show themselves. A few birds still sing languid late afternoon songs. A scarlet tanager's burry phrases carry through the darkening foliage. A wood-pewee's persistent whistle follows. Soon the nightjars and the owls will stir from their daytime roosts, ruffle their cryptically marked feathers, and set off on their nightly hunts. If I'm lucky I will hear their calls as they move through the dark forest, preying on certain diminutive mammals busy with their own nocturnal endeavors on the forest floor.

Perhaps I willed myself to be here. I don't know. As I stretch out on my cot and pick up a book I think about how far away I feel from where I just was. An over-whelming sense of peace pervades my being. The anxiety and dread clinging to me in the other place have dis-solved. It is true I am alone here. But I feel an untapped reservoir of energy from which to draw. Here I am not surrounded by those with faces like drains, as that one lyric goes. Here there is unspoiled life, everywhere one looks. It buoys me, carries my spirit aloft. The other place devitalizes me with cold efficiency. I wake up and as the hours tick by, my energy drops at an alarming rate. By day's end I am wrung out, sucked dry by the vampiric nature of existence inside that bubble. Here I still reach toward sleep out of exhaustion, but at least it feels honest and earned by my own hand.

3.

I wake the next morning in a panic, unwilling to open my eyes and discover where I am. Living on this precipice may destroy me. I must find a way to stabilize my existence. It would almost be preferable to lock in a life in the city than to forever straddle these two places, never knowing how long I will be in one of them. Holding my breath now, I crack open my eyes and the dim outline of the cabin's Spartan furnishings comes into view. I breathe out and relax.

The door that first brought me here may be the key, if only I were to find it again. But there would remain the problem of inexplicable, unplanned travel between both places, bypassing the door somehow. I must find E. I am convinced she holds the answer. The herbs she speaks of, the ones the professor disparages. Yes, an herbal solution sounds appealing.

For lack of any other plan I decide today to search for the door. I dress quickly, eat breakfast, and leave for the mainland. After a quick survey of the garden, I enter the cedar wood, breathing in its spicy-sweet aroma. I soon hear the rustling of raven wings and find comfort in the awareness of my dark companions over-head. I walk with soundless steps on fallen pine needles, passing through thick gnarled groves of rhododendron and mountain laurel. Here and there a patch of sunlight falls across my path. I do not know where I am going. I cannot recall what direction I walked in that day I found the door. Only the ravens know, and I have no idea if the ones accompanying me now are the same ones that showed me the way before. I must admit my hope is dwindling and I worry about traveling too deep into the woods. I have no compass and my time here in the past was short-lived. I never wandered far except on the day I found the door.

As if to encourage me the ravens croak back and forth to each other. Of course I am anthropomorphiz-ing their behavior in order to make myself feel better about what feels like a futile journey that may only serve to imperil me. One advantage to living in an enclosed city is the impossibility of getting lost. All tunnels lead somewhere, and virtually everyone knows what's at the end of each of them. But perhaps the inability to get lost blunts our curiosity. If I know where every route goes, I am more likely to only choose any given one if I need to get to what is at the end of it. As such, life collates itself into a series of purpose-driven trips to known destinations. The mind dulls and the body loses its flexibility. With each anticipated step the desire to continue flags. If I always know what is to come then why bother going at all.

Above me the ravens chuckle excitedly. Tuned to their urgency I look around, but of course see nothing through the rhododendron. I struggle to keep up with them as they begin moving through the treetops at an accelerated rate. Soon we emerge into a clearing. I cannot be certain, but it looks like the same clearing they led me to before. Unlike before, though, once I enter the clearing the ravens cease to show interest in either it or me. They circle around it once, emitting their strange gurgling calls, before flying off in silence.

Now I am at a loss. For one, I don't know if I will be able to find my way back to the lake's edge. But I set this concern aside for now and decide to explore the clearing. The sun is still climbing toward its midday altitude and looks to have at least a couple more hours to go. As I examine my surroundings more closely the first element I notice is the shape of the clearing. It appears to be a perfect circle, almost as if it has been purposefully created and maintained. The topography of the clearing is also of interest. It is bowl-shaped, with a slight grade all around gently descending to a low point, also circular, at the center. The ground cover consists primarily of moss and creeping phlox scattered among flat, lichen-covered rock.

I walk to the center of the clearing and pause to admire the pleasing view radiating in all directions: out to the ring of conifers at the forest edge, down to the lush green vegetative blanket at my feet, and up to the cloudless blue sky above. The space has an ancient, sacred feel to it. I don't think I took the time before to notice the beauty here. I did not have the time, I suppose, for as soon as I walked to the clearing's center, the door appeared, and without much deliberation, I walked straight through it.

Today, however, the door does not appear. Notwithstanding its few curious attributes and general otherworldly ambiance, the clearing offers up no secret portal or any other mysteries. Why the ravens brought me here will, for now at least, remain unknown. If they even had a purpose. Perhaps I am overzealous in my attribution of portentousness to their behavior. Or I'm merely mad. I think birds are trying to communicate with me, which could be a sign of mental instability. On the other hand, it could be indicative of advancement to a higher level of consciousness, which is how I would prefer to characterize my questionable behavior.

I leave the clearing from the point where I entered, which takes me a few minutes to locate after having stood at the clearing's center and rotated my body multiple times. Once under the cedar canopy, my shadow friends surprisingly return and travel with me, guiding my steps back toward the lake's edge. After finishing my work in the garden I return to the island. I don't feel like the morning was a loss. There is still something elusive about the clearing. Its magnetic power draws me to it. I know I will return there.

At the cabin I discover someone has been here in my absence. My few possessions are strewn around the room. I am baffled. For one, I have not seen a single other person during any of my time in this place. I had implicitly assumed the area was remote and uninhabited. Whoever it was must have come from the mainland and used the boat to cross and return while I was in the forest. Unless they remain on the island.

I rush outside and begin circumnavigating the tiny island. It is not easy, for the half of it behind my tiny homestead is densely wooded. I am wary of making too much noise in case the interloper remains on site. I spend several hours combing through the woods before giving up. By the time I return to the cabin I am reasonably convinced I am alone here. Inside I sit at the table and consider what someone may have wanted from me. I have nothing here beyond the rudimentary tools necessary for basic existence. The only things of possible value in my possession exist in my head: my knowledge of this place, how I got here, where I came from, who I am, who I know. I don't know who would want this knowledge, but it is all I can think of that someone might want. Realizing this unsettles me. As I lie on my cot, for the first time in this place I feel the anxiety and dread return.

4.

I am dreaming now. I'm in the tunnels, in the alcove, staring at the paintings. Suddenly E appears in front of me.

So do you like my work?

Ah, I knew it was yours.

Do you see here, how I lengthened the lines and darkened the centers?

She points to the painting from the textbook, the one I am sure I've seen somewhere before.

Yes...but why are you here. And why have you hung these in the tunnels?

She laughs. Well, there are no more art galleries, right?

Yes, but why. Why now? What does it mean?

Don't you get it? I'm trying to wake them up. I even brought F along to help. She's an artist, too.

She gestures to someone standing apart from her, in the shadows beyond the alcove. F walks forward and stands in the lurid glow of the sodium lamp.

Here she is. You two have met before, haven't you?

I stare at F. She does look familiar somehow, but I'm not sure.

Well, it's not important, not now anyway. Did you get my message from N?

Sort of. The professor refused to translate it. He only told me you thought you'd found a cure for the condition.

She rolls her eyes. Oh, that man. He has caused me more trouble than I can tell you about now. Let's just say he's not exactly on our side, if you know what I mean.

But...I don't. I don't know what you mean. I don't know what's going on. Can't you see that? I need your help.

She laughs. Oh, so now you need my help. What about all the time I spent trying to help you before I left? Does that not count for anything?

It does. I'm sorry. I didn't know what I was doing then.

You're still a mess, aren't you?

No, I'm not. I'm better than I was. The blackouts, they've stopped. I have a new project at work—it's not nearly as mind-numbing.

She sighs. What have I told you about talking about work? Will you ever learn? Honestly, I'm not sure you will.

244 | S. D. Stewart

I look helplessly at F who is now gazing at the paintings behind us. She is tiny—ephemeral as a ghost. I suddenly feel faint as I see her there juxtaposed in front of the paintings. She peers closer at the one of the tree. Its orange bark appears to be glowing, as if E used phosphorescent paint to accentuate it in the darkness of the tunnel.

E snaps her fingers in front of my face. Hey, are you okay?

I-I'm not sure. I may be having one of my spells.

I thought you said the blackouts stopped.

Well, they had. Until now, I guess.

Quite a coincidence that you're having one now, right when we show up. Are you sure you're not dreaming? Should I pinch you?

I laugh weakly. My vision is getting grainy, or maybe it's just the poor light in the tunnels. I can't tell. I thought I was sitting down, but I'm not and now I feel my legs growing unsteady.

Well, it's been nice catching up, but we've got to be on our way.

Wait, you're leaving...

Yes, that's what I said. We have work to do, F and I.

Lots of work. And so little time! Especially since F is only here for so long.

What do you mean? Where is she going?

Don't worry about that. I'm sure we'll see you again soon. Or at least I will. I'll always be around, you know. I can't say the same for F. She comes and goes, you know.

No...I don't know. Wait, please don't go. I need more answers.

I'm sure you do. But I don't have them for you. That is not the kind of help I offer. Now, don't worry. You'll be fine. We'll catch up later.

She walks off with F trailing behind her.

Wait!

F looks back at me, a faint smile on her lips.

I black out and when I wake up I hear the artificial birds, each of them singing a different song.

5.

As I grow more aware of my surroundings I hear a noise from the anteroom. Someone is in my quarters. I rise silently and creep toward the door. Peering out, I see the professor sitting on the settee drinking a cup of tea. He looks up at me.

Ah, you're awake.

What are you doing here?

Well, I found you passed out in the mailroom a few hours ago. So I had the concierge help me bring you up here.

The mailroom...

Yes, do you remember being in there?

I'm not sure. But you can leave now. Thank you for your assistance.

He puts down his cup and looks at me.

Look, I know we've had our differences. But I assure you I only have the best intentions.

What does that even mean? Intentions regarding what?

He sighs. If you don't know, then perhaps I am wasting my time on you.

Good lord, man. Could you be even more cryptic? I'm sick of it.

I think I should go. You're obviously upset. I'm sure it's been a great strain on you, this experience. I don't want to make it any harder.

I consider forcing him to stay. I want to interrogate him, squeeze out of him whatever he is holding back. But it feels pointless. I get the sense he is a dead end. I am surrounded by these dead ends.

I open the door and gesture for him to leave.

Have a nice night, professor. Thanks again, but next time just leave me wherever you find me.

He winces, but says nothing. I shut the door, carry his cup to the kitchen, and sit down at the table. Out of habit I pick up the electro-syringe and inject myself with a shot of vitamin D. I can no longer keep track of what has been lost. I feel nothing. I am so tired of feeling nothing.

6.

The next morning I go to work. I'm slumped in my chair when N arrives, cheery as always. She sits down across from me.

Good morning! I captioned and tagged the last batch of images you sent me.

Thanks. I should have another batch for you later this morning.

Okay. How are you feeling?

I've been better.

Do you want to tell me about it?

I shift in my seat. I must tread carefully here. I cannot say too much, despite my urge to unburden myself once and for all. When in doubt, then, answer a question with a question...

Do you remember your dreams?

Sometimes. But I don't dream much. I drink this herbal infusion before I go to sleep. It inhibits dreaming.

How do you know about that?

E told me. She gave me a supply before I came here. Remember, we know each other from the other city.

Oh, right. But I thought you didn't even believe the condition exists.

I don't think I said that exactly. I said it seems like people use it as an excuse not to connect with others. But it could be real. After all, you believe you have it. And whether it exists or not, it can't hurt to take some herbs just in case. Don't you take them?

No.

Why not? Didn't E ever tell you to? I would have thought she had.

My agitation begins to grow. No, she didn't tell me.

Huh. That's strange. It seems like you two were pretty close, so I just figured...

We were close, in a way. But in other ways we were far apart. If that makes sense.

Yeah, I guess so.

Was E recording your dreams in the other city? Is that how you met her?

No, I met her at a coffeehouse. I told you that. Don't you remember?

Ah, I do now. Sorry. I have these memory problems.

Has E ever filmed your dreams?

I laugh. Mine? No.

Why is that funny?

It's not, really. I was just imagining what she would think if she saw my dreams.

Why, are they terrible?

Sometimes. Well, maybe not terrible. But more like frightening in how realistic they are.

What do you dream about?

At that moment, I see my superior pass by the open door. I suspect he's lingering to speak with me.

Excuse me, N. I think the boss needs a word with me.

She turns around, sees the man loitering in the hallway.

Oh, sure. Well, just send me that batch of photos when they're ready. I don't have much else to do right now.

Will do.

She leaves and my boss enters.

How are the numbers looking?

We're on schedule. N is working out great. I've been reviewing her work and it's at a level where I think she'll be okay on her own now.

Good to hear. So, you'll be submitting the first quarter's report soon?

I'll have it to you tomorrow.

Great.

There's an awkward pause during which he looks around the room.

So, everything else okay? You feeling alright?

I force a smile. I'm fine. Why is everyone so concerned about my health?

Oh, c'mon. You know you've had some...issues. I just want to make sure you're feeling up to this project. If we do well on this initial short-term contract, our liaison officer has hinted there might be more contracts in the pipeline we could lock in. This could really put us in good shape for the next few years.

That's good to hear. And I assure you I am up to it. No worries on this end.

Excellent. I will leave you to it then.

He leaves and I feel myself wilting. The sheer amount of energy required to sustain those two conversations has left me wasted. I will not survive this project, never mind another few years. It's absurd I am even here at all, in this position, after so long. I do not belong here, and I have no idea how I have deceived everyone else into thinking I do.

7.

I go to the coffeehouse and read E's letter again. I don't know why I keep reading it, what I hope to find in or between its lines. It does not ever offer up any new information. As far as I can tell there is no encoded message within it. E sounds disillusioned—with her vocation, with the professor, with life in general. Even her description of the artwork she is doing is laced with desperation. If she was so unhappy in that other city I don't know why she would have come back here, if she even has. It seems like being in this place again would only agitate all the issues she writes about.

I look around the shop. The coffeehouse regulars never change. A few of them even nod at me now when I arrive. I am part of their accepted reality. I am expected. My presence is not an aberration. They may wonder where my companion is, though. Why she never comes here anymore. She probably stuck in their minds more than I ever did. E is a much more memorable individual. Her blue hair alone is enough to register her in someone's mind. I, on the other hand, have no distinguishing characteristics. Perhaps it is why I cannot seem to root myself anywhere. I am indistinguishable from the faceless masses moving through the tunnels. I could be any of them.

After work I return exhausted to my quarters. I am too tired even to cook dinner so I make a cup of tea. While waiting for the water to boil, I wander restlessly through my rooms. I notice the drawer where I keep my dream book is slightly ajar. I slide it open and take out the journal. There is no evidence it's been tampered with, but someone still could have read it. I am certain I did not leave the drawer ajar. It is not something I would do. The professor could have, though. While I was passed out he may have rifled through my quarters. Apparently he was in here for several hours until I woke up. Perhaps I made a noise or rolled over, startling him, and he quickly replaced the book and in his haste did not shut the drawer all the way. It seems a likely explanation. Or maybe I am just indulging in paranoia again.

The chamomile tea works its magic, though tonight I do not need much help. I lie down on the bed and try to quell the dread creeping through my body. I stare at the never-changing light outside the window. The artificial birds begin their song, but their program has developed an inoperable error. They no longer all sing the same song. Now it is not just one bird carrying a different tune, but all of them, and all in different keys. It is a horrid sound, much worse than the original sound of them all singing in perfect harmony, which though monotonous, was at least designed to be easy to tune out. But it is impossible to ignore this cacophony. I struggle to block it out until my exhaustion overwhelms me and I cross the border into sleep.

8.

I am outside. Out in the wasteland where there are no birds at all. The only sound here is the blustering wind. Ahead of me two figures crouch in the swirling dust, their backs to me, their heads just touching. I know without looking closer who they are. I know too what they are doing. I don't know how I know this but I can see it. They are preparing the way, sketching with their fingers in the dust. They have my journal and they are drawing what they find in it, the lines disappearing as soon as they complete them. A perfect set of lines.

One of them—the one who is almost translucent—turns toward me and beckons. What can I do but approach. I reach their position and kneel down between them. What I see is not how I imagined it, but who among us would recognize their own dream sketched out in dust. My two companions link arms with me and for a moment we are as one. I lie down then across the fading lines of my dream, stretching out my limbs as far as I can in the four directions, and still myself as the dust begins to cover me.

ACKNOWLEDGMENTS

With gratitude to Nate Dorr, Reuben Andrews, and Nathan Grover for reading various drafts and providing invaluable feedback. You all made this a better story.

Special thanks to Nate Dorr for the stunning cover and illustrations and to Nathan Grover for his mad design skills.

Thank you also to the band Nadja, whose music provided aural inspiration during the initial drafting.